A Christmas Blizzard

Garrison Keillor

THORNDIKE PRESS
A part of Gale, Cengage Learning

Detroit • New York • San Francisco • New Haven, Conn • Waterville, Maine • London

Thorndike Press, a part of Gale, Cengage Learning.

Thorndike Press® Large Print Core.

The text of this Large Print edition is unabridged.

Other aspects of the book may vary from the original edition.

Set in 16 pt. Plantin.

Printed on permanent paper.

LIBRARY OF CONGRESS CATALOGING-IN-PUBLICATION DATA

Keillor, Garrison.
A Christmas blizzard / by Garrison Keillor.
p. cm.
ISBN-13: 978-1-4104-2306-1 (hardcover : alk. paper)
ISBN-10: 1-4104-2306-9 (hardcover : alk. paper)
1. Travelers —Fiction. 2. Blizzards —Fiction. 3. North Dakota —Fiction 4. Christmas stories. 5. Large type books.
I. Title.
PS3561.E3755C48 2009b
813'.54—dc22

2009040052

Published in 2009 by arrangement with Viking, a member of Penguin Group (USA) Inc.

Printed in the United States of America
1 2 3 4 5 6 7 13 12 11 10 09

A Christmas Blizzard

1. James Sparrow awakens too early and is besieged by the mean Christmas blues

It was an old familiar nightmare, the one about men in black hoods chasing him through tall grass toward the precipice overlooking jagged rocks and great greenish waves rolling and crashing in the abyss where sharks with chainsaw teeth awaited and great black buzzards hung in the air and there he was sliding toward extinction and then Mr. Sparrow woke up to a song emanating from somewhere close to the bed —

When he plays his drum, pa-rum-

pum-pum-pum,
Let's break his thumbs

He thought maybe it was part of the dream, the masked men torturing him with a Christmas carol before tossing him to the sharks, and he lay waiting for the dream to evaporate, *poof,* so he could restart his sleep, but it was still there, that Christmas song he loathed and despised:

I played my drum for Him, pa-rum-
pum-pum-pum
He told me, Beat it, Jim, pa-rum-
pum-pum-pum

It was dark except for a faint glow from the bathroom. He was in Chicago. Mrs. Sparrow lay asleep next to him in their emperor-size bed in the hushed splendor of the master bedroom in their baronial twelve-room apartment on the 55th floor of the Wabasha Tower, and it was December 22. In two days, the red-green monster of Christmas would descend. The World's Longest & Unhappiest Holiday. Mrs. Sparrow adored Christmas and Mr. Sparrow dreaded it. It gave him the heebie-jeebies. It gave him the hives. The brass quintets tooting "God Rest Ye Merry, Gentlemen" on street corners and the sugar-plum fairies twirling in the windows of Marshall Field and inside, in women's lingerie, a pianist plowed through the little town of Bethlehem like a backhoe digging a ditch. It was ubiquitous, inescapable, the smell of pine and the bullying ads and the germs of guilt — *you did not buy Christmas gifts for all the people you should have and the gifts were not nice enough.* You could fly off to Hawaii — and Mr. Sparrow was hoping to do just that — but you could not drive Christmas away, it was a dark fog of nostalgia and disappointment that gripped you like a vise.

"Oh darling Joyce, Oh Joyce my love, let's away to the warm Pacific and float in the star-spangled sea," he said to her one week ago. "We'll see," she said. He groaned. "I'll check my schedule," she said. He groaned again. The snow and the cold, the bleakness of light, and the sheer horror of "The Little Drummer Boy" coming at you when you least expected it, *pa-rum-pum-pum-pum.* Mrs. Sparrow attended two *Nutcracker*s every year, two *Messiah*s, and three *A Christmas*

Carols, she loved Christmas so much (and also she served on the Boards of Directors of the ballet and the symphony and the theater). Mr. Sparrow wished that the mice would carry Clara away and lock her in a dungeon and that the *Hallelujah Chorus* could be embargoed for ten years and that Tiny Tim would learn a useful trade and quit blessing people. Poor Mr. Dickens and the juggernaut he had wrought. Back when he wrote about Scrooge and the nebbishy Cratchits, Christmas was a one-day event, like Valentine's Day or Memorial Day, and you did the thing on that day and it was over, but his little book created a rage of Christmas, and it spread out of control, and now the good man would be horrified to see it. The incessant dinging of bells.

The godawful music seeping out of cracks in ceilings like liquid gas. The anguished jollity of store clerks living in the hell of holiday shopping. The invitations to parties where people who don't like each other stand cheek by jowl at a downtown club and get glassy-eyed on Artillery punch. Mr. Sparrow's company, Coyote Corp., did not do Christmas parties. His 325 employees were sent nice bonus checks and given a week off but nothing to do with Christmas, thank you very much. There was no glittery tree in the lobby, no wreaths, no candles.

He hoisted himself up on one elbow and gazed at her, earplugs in place, his true love in her cardigan sweater, soft purple pants, and red socks, and groped for the bedside lamp and knocked a book off the stack on the bedside table and also his eyedrops and almost spilled a glass of juice. Mrs. Sparrow turned over but did not open her eyes. He put the glass to his lips and — *pfffffeh!!!!!!!!!!* — cranberry juice! Simon had left him a glass of *cranberry* juice. Why? The mere taste of it brought back bitter memories, the boredom of breast of turkey, the big yawn of yams, the pointlessness of pumpkin.

Said the shepherd to the little lamb,
I have a gift to bring, pa-rum-pum-pum-pum
A noose and scaffolding, pa-rum-pum-pum-pum.

It was the digital clock radio Simon had installed that Mr. Sparrow had never figured out. The thing cost

$14,000, an iClock with an eRadio and a pPhone (with videocam) that could access bank accounts, activate a coffeemaker, download a newspaper, start a robot vacuum cleaner or trouser press, open up e-mail and have it read to you in a pleasant Australian female voice who would also say your schedule for the day *(9 A.M. you have a breakfast meeting with Mr. Jeepers. Here. At Wabasha Towers. This concerns tax liability.),* and if you wished to change the schedule you could get the Australian lady to call Mr. Jeepers' voice mail and deliver the message *(This is a recorded message from Mr. James Sparrow. He is very sorry but he is forced to cancel your breakfast meeting today at 9 A.M. He apologizes for any inconvenience this may cause and he will be in touch with you as soon as possible. Thank you, and have a wonderful day.)* It was a marvelous device, made by BRB Inc., a wholly owned subsidiary of Mr. Sparrow's Coyote Corp., and he didn't know how to turn it off as it played him Christmas music that made him faintly ill.

I wish this song were done, pa-rum-
pum-pum-pum
Go get my gun . . .

"So what do you want for Christmas?" she asked him two days ago, having forgotten what he'd said about the Pacific.

"Hawaii," he said. "All I want for Christmas is warmth and sunshine. I am desperate for sunlight. The freedom of walking out the door in your shorts and T-shirt and into a warm and welcoming atmosphere. You feel the same way. Admit it. So let's go. The plane is gassed up and ready to go."

"Oh darling, why can't we wait until the week after Christmas?"

The truth was, Joyce was uneasy about the luxury, having grown up frugal in Wauwatosa, Wisconsin. She felt bad about the fuel consumption of the company jet, the eight-passenger twin-engine (4000-lb. thrust) Conquistador 409 named the *Lucky Lady.* "Don't think about it," he said, but she did; she sat grim-faced in that beautiful pale leather (1000-cu.-ft.) interior of the plane and he knew she was thinking they should've invited some disadvantaged children to come with them, so as to justify the expense. He did not care to have disadvantaged children with him in Hawaii. He had been disadvantaged himself and now, as a recovering disadvantaged child, he had learned to enjoy pleasure, actually *enjoy* it, not merely tolerate it, waiting for the other shoe to drop. Mrs. Sparrow, on the other hand, definitely did *not* like to be waited on by old black men in starched white uniforms and she fretted about the fresh-cut flowers in all the rooms and about food waste and how much they were paying for this 1997 Pinot Noir with elegant structure and an extended palate, complex and bright on a tannic frame, nicely oaked with a lingering finish of boysenberries, sheepskin, and pencil shavings, and what that money could do if you spent it on digging wells for African villages which didn't have any.

And then that night they had a big stupid argument about going to her family's for Christmas. So yesterday, hoping to make up with her, he dragged himself through Marshall Field looking at velveteen cocktail dresses and bright blouses and silk pantaloons, thinking, *Anything I like, she won't. Guaranteed. So give up.* He looked at a miniature Swiss village made of porcelain with clock tower and church steeple and people sliding down a hill on tiny toboggans and couples skating on a pond. Looked at books. Big luxurious picture books. *The Twentieth Century in Pictures.* He opened it. And then closed it. What does a beautiful woman need to know about the wretched mistakes of great men and the insanity of war? The past is over and done and let's dance on into the future.

He stopped in the music department and a boy with four earrings in each ear, and a strange hairdo like a small animal crouched on top of his head asked, "Are you looking for something?" and James guessed he was not. He looked at digital cameras, telescopes on tripods, a long-haired sheepskin from New Zealand, luxurious white turkish bathrobes and cosmetics, where a woman with skin the color of oiled almond spritzed a liquid on a card and rubbed some on the back of his hand for him to smell and whispered, "For whom are you shopping today?" and James said, "For a woman I love who I had a fight with." The almond-skinned woman smiled and said, "This will do, then." And he bought it. For almost a thousand dollars. An ounce of something called PH.

He clicked a switch on the console and the wall opposite the bed lit up with a bright projection of a map of Chicago and a blinking light at 59th and Cicero where *Lucky Lady* was parked at Midway Airport. He could call Simon, asleep in the servant's wing, and have him call up the driver Ramon and the pilots Buzz and Buddy and the plane could be airborne in two hours. But he could not, could not, could not, turn off the song. He was upright now, feet on the floor, looking for the light switch. The iClock said 5:42 A.M. He poked some dark circles on the touch pad and a different song came on:

Starlight moonlight

All alone, thinking about you
When a man loves a woman, Lord,
Lord, what can he do?

It was the Moondog show on AM77 which sometimes in bouts of insomnia he tuned in for a fitful hour or two to hear the Moondog talk about Fanny May and how she tormented him with her passionate ways followed by tears of regret and then long passages of indifference. He poked the pad again.

Adeste fideles
Laeti triumphantes . . .

He knelt down on the floor to search for the plug and snaked his hand far under the bed but couldn't reach the outlet. The choir was calling for the faithful to come, which brought back painful memories of Christmas growing up in Looseleaf, North Dakota — of the scrawny Christmas tree and Mother worried it would burst into flames and they would die in their sleep of smoke inhalation and Daddy worried that Mother would spend them into bankruptcy and they would have to go live in a public institution and wear orange jumpsuits and pick up trash along the highway.

Gonna lay my head on the railroad line
And let the longest train I ever saw come and pacify my mind
'Cause the water tastes like turpentine
And I can't keep from cryin'
And the nations so furiously rage

against me.

"Darling?" he said in a clear voice. "Darling —" She opened her eyes, the comforter pulled up to her chin, her dark hair splayed against the pillow. She pulled an earplug out.

"How do you turn this music off?" She looked up at him in wonderment. So he repeated the question.

"It's voice controlled. You just say *OFF.*" And the music stopped.

2. Unpleasant memories of the joyous season

"What time is it?" she said.

"Almost six o'clock."

"Why?"

"It just is. I'm sorry I woke you. Go back to sleep."

"I can't." She sat up. "God, I am so sick. Some horrible flu virus. I was sitting next to this blowhard at the meeting of the ballet board and he was sneezing all over me. No hanky, nothing — just leaned back and barked and let fly with thousands of tiny beads of infection flying in the air."

"You'd feel better if we went to

Hawaii."

"Oh darling, you go — it's okay. I can't bear the thought of getting on a plane. I am sick to my stomach."

And with that, she threw off the covers and leaped toward the bathroom in three bounds and slammed the door and he heard water running in the sink and other more visceral sounds and he was transported back to the terrible Christmas when the Dark Angel of Projectile Vomiting visited them. Oh my gosh, what a vivid memory it was. Twenty-five years ago and still he could feel the gorge rising in the pit of his stomach, the acid bubbling up, the muscles tightening. He was 17 and that day in school he had suffered the most harrowing humiliation of his life, standing in front of twenty leering choir members as Miss Forsberg said, "Tenors, open your mouths, you can't sing with your mouths shut. Basses, read the notes. They're right in front of you." And nodded to him and he started to sing, "Why do the nations so furiously rage together," and what came out was *Wfmrghghghgh* and the sopranos screeched like hyenas, and Miss Forsberg said, "Again!" and he screwed it up again. Choked. He slunk home from choir, running the gauntlet of snowballers — and in Looseleaf, the snowballs were *hard* and thrown sidearm with deadly accuracy — and he found Mother making the stuffing to put in the turkey and weeping over their imminent deaths which she could see clearly:

FAMILY OF FIVE DIES IN CHRIST-

MAS EVE FIRE;
FAULTY WIRING FINGERED AS CAUSE;
CHRISTMAS TREE LIGHTS EXPLODED AROUND 2 A.M.;
RESCUERS UNABLE TO FIGHT WAY THROUGH FLAMES;
PITIFUL SHRIEKS HEARD FROM UPSTAIRS BEDROOM;
NEIGHBORS PLACE MEMORIAL WREATHS AT SITE;
"A NICE FAMILY," SAYS ONE, "KEPT TO THEMSELVES BUT ALWAYS FRIENDLY AND WILLING TO HELP."

Mother checked the Christmas tree frequently for signs of combustion and he tried to tell her that he wanted to quit choir forever as she poured fresh water into the tree stand and snapped off dry branches. Meanwhile Daddy was ranting and raving about money. "I will never understand to the end of my born days," he said, "how someone can leave a room without turning off the light. How much exertion does it take to reach up and snap off a light switch? You must think we are Hollywood stars made of money to see this house with lights blazing at night."

Mother heard the word "blazing" and shuddered at the thought. A Christmas tree blazing up and burning down your house. The irony of it: you bring a thing of beauty and magic into your home, and it turns around and kills you. The lights left on too long, the tree not properly watered, the family exhausted from the festivities, and in the wee hours — *poof!* spontaneous combustion! A deadly conflagration. The family vaporized.

She felt weak in the knees and had to sit down. And then felt sick to her stomach.

Daddy looked at the stack of presents under the tree and cried out, "You've gone mad! You must think I am made of money! What possessed you, woman? I am only a municipal employee. I am not Santa Claus."

And that was the year she gave James a dictionary for Christmas that had been owned by someone else. He was hoping for a telescope, a pair of Bass Weejuns, sunglasses, a transistor radio, a pair of cords, but he got a used dictionary. Wrapped up in used Christmas wrapping with old creases in it. A used dictionary and inside you could see where someone had erased the words *Monique, Happy Birthday*. He showed it to Mother and she said,

"Oh." That was all she said. *Oh.*

Projectile vomiting was going on upstairs in the little frame house and the smell of Lysol was heavy in the air. Elaine and Benny were sicker than dogs, moaning in their twin beds, feverish, achy, nauseated, a basin by the bed into which they yorked up their Rye-Krisp and ginger ale. James stood in the door and told them to forget about Christmas. "You expect Santa to come and get your germs and spread them to every other boy and girl on this planet so that there is a mass epidemic of vomiting and diarrhea all over the world? What sort of Christmas would that be? Santa coming down the chimney and leaving your germs and the boys and girls wake up in the morning in a pool of green poop? Of course Santa isn't going to come. Forget about it." They put their hot little faces into their pillows and sobbed heart-wrenching sobs and he went downstairs and soon began to feel queasy.

And just then, as he heard Mother pour buttermilk into a bowl to make custard, the Dark Angel touched his shoulder and he had to dash to the bathroom — and the door was locked. He knocked. Daddy said, "Go away." So he had to dash outdoors and there, in the snow, it exploded out of him at both ends. Oh my. Oh dear. Stomach and bowels. Chunks of many colors. He scooped up snow to hide the disgrace but it soaked right in. He took off his pants and heaved them out into the dark, into a deep snowbank, and washed himself with snow, and snuck into the house full of Christmas lights and radio choirs and slunk up to his bed and spent two days of invalidism, lying very quietly, not eating anything or thinking about eating or wanting to hear about anybody eating, feeling like the object of a cruel experiment.

It was very quiet. He knocked on the bathroom door. "Are you all right?" There was a groan from inside. "Would you like a ginger ale? Some toast and tea?"

"No," she said. She opened the door. She had washed her face and she looked up at him all beautiful and needy and he put his arms around her. "There's no need to suffer," he said. "How about I call a doctor?"

"No need to waste a doctor's time. It's the common flu, darling, or whatever that jerk was passing around. I guess I'll just stay in bed for Christmas."

He was going to say something about Hawaii and alternative medicine and decided not to. He put on a robe and walked barefoot across the thick gray angora carpet. A mirror hung on the wall and he ducked it. Didn't want to see his face just now. His bland face with the light green, almost yellowish, eyes — "gecko eyes," cousin Liz called them when they were kids. And into the hallway overlooking Lake Michigan and past the library and the dining room into the kitchen and out onto the terrace. Snow was falling. His big oak hot tub sat by the railing. He pulled off the insulated cover and steam boiled up into the cold air. The floating thermometer said 110 degrees. He stripped off his pajamas and climbed in and sat, water up to his chin, snow falling on his head, and looked out into the darkness of the lake and thought about Hawaii. The sheer beauty of their estate at Kuhikuhikapapa'u'maumau — and how, after a day or two, the sheer tranquility of the house and grounds worked its wonders on them. Some evenings, they would walk down the great lawn to the beach and drop their robes and walk naked into the sea and swim out a hundred yards and float there as the sun went down, to see the lights come on in the great house and the lanai and the portico around the pool, an ivory palace under the sheltering palms, as they floated in the arms of the everlasting sea, inhaling the salt air and the sweet blossomy breeze, listening to the chef's little daughter play her one Chopin étude and the two of them transcended the Midwest and entered into a state of buoyant blessedness.

3. A brief background on how he came to acquire his enormous fortune

He was not sleeping well these days — ironic, considering that his financial empire was built from an energy drink called 4xPrime made from ionized chlorophyll from coyote grass; a broad-stemmed plant devoured by coyotes during mating season, that, to put it simply, gives you high energy and focus from dawn to midnight and then the equivalent of eight hours of sleep in just two hours. 4xPrime swept like prairie fire through the professional and managerial ranks in the late 1990s, word of mouth, no ads, completely under the media radar, a secret greenish liquid that millions of people knew about — a few drops in your coffee or tea and you were a monster of productivity. It didn't work for everybody. Maybe only 20 percent of 4xPrime consumers got the full benefit, but for those people, it was rocket fuel. They worked late into the night and napped and awoke before dawn feeling fresh and ambitious and showed up at the 7:00 A.M. meeting full of fresh brilliance and maintained a killer pace all day and took home a briefcase bulging with work and delivered it in the morning all tidy and polished and never complained. All thanks to a grass that coyote eat to give them stamina to flirt and skitter and howl at the moon. The Sioux warriors who ate Custer's lunch were tanked up on coyote grass.

James bought the formula for $1250 from an old chemist in the Wrangler Saloon in Livingston, Montana. The man was in his cups and falling off the barstool and James was on the road selling aluminum shelving and peanut brittle. He was 32 and had no bright prospects in life, he was stumbling along from one budget motel to the next, a life of discolored TVs and lumpy beds and breakfast rooms with a ten-gallon dispenser of Cheerios and stale sweet rolls and bitter coffee. That fall, in South Dakota, he bought a ski mask and took up bank robbery, which he liked. There was stress, of course, and a constant fear of failure — you thrust the note at the teller ("Yes, you're right. This is a robbery. Don't push that alarm button and nobody gets hurt. Put all your money in this bag and hand it over. Nice and slow. And then go to the bathroom and stay there for one half hour.") and what if she laughed in your face and told you to take a hike? The "gun" in your pocket was nothing but a corn cob. On the other hand, the money was good and you kept banker's hours. And there was plenty of time off between jobs. So there was the good and the bad. He had robbed banks in Mitchell, Pierre, Rapid City, and Billings, and was in Livingston to pull one more bank job and while he sat in his car in the parking lot, the ski mask on top of his head, composing the note, two men galloped into the bank wearing Halloween masks, pistols in hand. Their eyeholes must've been not lined up right because they ran right into a sculpture of a boy and his dog — one hit the boy, the other the dog — and whacked themselves in the groin and fell limp and helpless to the marble floor where a female security guard sprayed them with pepper spray. The sheer humiliation of it — to run around in Donald Duck masks and have your gonads dinged by a work of art and then get a shot of pepper in the snoot. James Sparrow gave up bank robbery in that minute. He threw away the mask and ripped up the note and went to the bar to celebrate when the old chemist leaned over and breathed on him and asked for a loan. James gave him a ten-dollar bill. The drunk looked at it and burst into tears and pulled out the formula, scrawled in pencil on Holiday Inn stationery, and offered it to him for a hundred bucks. "This is great stuff to put the lead in your pencil," he said. The man had been fired after thirty-two years at Monsanto. He was on his way to Tucson to see his sister Kathy, he said.

"You can't get to Tucson on a hundred bucks."

The man said he had enough money for a Greyhound ticket. "They gave me a nice severance package."

"Where's your stuff?"

The man pointed with his right foot at a small red knapsack on the floor.

"That's it? That's all you got?"

He nodded.

James got Kathy's phone number from him. He called Greyhound and bought the ticket and called her and told her to pick up her brother Wednesday morning at 11:30 A.M. and handed him $1,250. He had enough dough, he thought it would be good luck to share. The man wept. He made James take the formula. James said, "I've got no use for that," but the man insisted. "The world needs this," he said. "That's my baby. You take good care of her." He slipped the paper into James's pocket. And he picked up the knapsack and tottered out the door more or less in the direction of the depot. James took the formula to a lab in Chicago and, after some trial and error — part of the formula had been lost to whiskey stains — they came up with a compound that seemed to work. James marketed it through the Internet back when the Net was like a secret society, and within a year he had a factory in Antigua going full-steam and a mailroom with fifty employees shipping the packages out by the truckload. Oddly, 4xPrime had little or no effect on James. It only made him gloomy.

A chance meeting with a whiskey-soaked chemist in a redneck bar in Livingston, Montana, a pool game in the background, a wiry guy with a cigarette on his lower lip and smoke in his face lining up a shot and Waylon Jennings singing about rainy-day women and a couple of them hanging around the pool game, and some scrawls on a motel notepad, and there was the start of Chapter 2 of his life, along with his hiring of some smart marketing people and a wizard accountant, and then he met Joyce and married her, and America poured money on his head, and now he was cruising at a comfortable altitude in life, and if he ran into turbulence, he could retreat to his Hawaiian estate, Kuhikuhikapapa'u'maumau, a hundred acres walled off on the leeward side of Lanai, the old plantation house and guest house and his studio and the beach house and the pool, surrounded by fragrant frangipani trees, with a thousand yards of white beach. You could swim in the morning and around one o'clock, Angelique would appear with iced mint tea and crab-cake sandwiches, and fresh sliced mango. In the afternoon, you lay in a cord hammock, napping, reading, amusing yourself, and nothing bad ever happened. Nothing. It wasn't even an option.

4. A rocky beginning to a difficult day

He walked through the long dark living room and across the pale maple floor of the kitchen that faced north toward Lincoln Park and got the urge to pack his bags and run. The sadness of blank windows of the Hancock Tower nearby. The headlights of cars on the Outer Drive heading for the salt mines and slaughterhouse. The red flasher of a chopper whumping overhead, probably taking a fat man with chest pains to the ER. A life of pork roasts coming home to roost. Black curtains drawn on the

55th floor of the Winfrey: probably in mourning for a loved one. The city lay under a thick blanket of clouds and he could feel the cold steel gates of winter closing down on him. He opened the cupboard and pulled out a package of rice cakes.

"Is everything all right, sir?" He jerked, his neck almost snapped. Simon had a bad habit of padding up silently behind him and barking. "Sorry, sir, didn't mean to startle you." *Embarrassing.* The rice cakes were strewn all over the kitchen floor. He checked his pajamas to make sure he hadn't wet himself.

"If you're hungry, sir, I can whip you up a little omelet. Egg whites and low-fat cheese and salsa. Cranberry juice."

"No thank you. And I wouldn't

mind if you poured that cranberry juice down the drain."

"It's good for the urinary tract, sir."

"My urinary tract is good enough for the purpose."

"Yes, sir. Of course."

Simon was picking up the rice cakes. "I've packed everything for the trip if you want to get an early start. The plane is ready, sir. It'll take Buzz and Buddy no more than half an hour to be ready for take-off."

"Mrs. Sparrow is under the weather."

"I have two doctors on call. One here and one at Kuhikuhikapapa'u'maumau. And by the way, you may not want to read the paper this morning, sir."

"No?"

"It's that little pushing incident two days ago on the street."

"You're joking. The jerk in the Santa Claus suit?"

"Don't trouble yourself over it. These things blow over. A day or two and it's all chaff in the wind, sir."

"Let me see it."

"Let the lawyers deal with it. You get on the plane and fly to Kuhikuhikapapa'u'maumau and have yourself a good time. Relax in the sun. Have a massage under the kamehamuhikana trees. Smell the hanihani bushes. Drink your dandelion-burdock juice. You'll be a new man."

"Hand over the paper, Simon."

Mr. Sparrow had had his jousts with the press before. When you are worth $230 million, it is more or less inevitable that someone will want to pee on your parade. But the encounter on the street outside Marshall Field was so minor, so nothing, he couldn't believe it had made its way into the *Tribune* and yet there he was, just below the fold, in full color, looking smirky and arrogant and ticked off, coming out of the Bunyan Club on Michigan Avenue, heading for his town car, a buxom young woman trailing him — Sophie, his marketing person, they'd just had lunch, but the picture suggests far, far more — and the photographer had just yelled at him, "Hey, Bird Man, how about a big cheesy grin?" and he turned to see who the yahoo was, and there's the picture. And alongside it —

CHI-TOWN TYCOON SHOVES SANTA WHO DARED ASK HIM TO UP GIFT, AND

SANTA SLAPS HIM WITH SUIT FOR $3 MILLION FOR MENTAL DISTRESS

It all started when Ronald M. Lavoris, 37, decided to change his life as a homeless derelict and attend AA and get a job and join Salem Free Covenant Church. In six months, he was scarcely recognizable to those who had known him as "Humbug" on the streets of the North Side. "It's all thanks to Jesus Christ who came into my life and made me His own," said Mr. Lavoris yesterday. "And that's why I was out bell-ringing for the Salvation Army. I was trying to make a difference."

And that was when he encountered James Sparrow, the founder and president of Coyote Corp., makers of 4xPrime, the food additive that has come under increasing scrutiny recently from the FDA. Mr. Sparrow was emerging from Marshall Field with $14,000 worth of purchases in two large shopping bags when Mr. Lavoris, ringing his bell vigorously, inadvertently rang it too close to Mr. Sparrow, who uttered a common Anglo-Saxon profanity.

"I don't think Christmas season is a time for people to be talking trash," said Mr. Lavoris. "So I told him so. And I asked him for a contribution. Anything at all. And he reached into his coat pocket and pulled out a dollar and dropped it in the pot. I couldn't believe that a man wearing a black cashmere coat that had to have cost upwards of four or five grand would be so cheap and I told him so and he shoved me."

Spokespersons for Coyote Corp. had no comment and declined to make Mr. Sparrow available for interviews.

"My world just sort of shattered at that moment. I felt as if I had done everything a man could do to pull himself up by his bootstraps and here a prominent Chicagoan dared to disrespect me in public and walk away from it. I threw my bell into a trash can and I took the money out of the pot and I went into the nearest cocktail lounge and I sat there in my Santa suit and I tied one on like never before. I started on beer and I went to whiskey and had Rusty Nails and Singapore Slings and White Russians until my wife came and found me and shoveled me into rehab. I am a shattered man. I forgive Mr. Sparrow for his assault on me but I do feel the man needs to be taught a lesson."

Mr. Lavoris said that, if the suit is successful, he would donate all of the award, minus legal expenses, to Salem Free Covenant Church to build a gymnasium for neighborhood children.

"See?" said Simon. "I told you not to read it."

"I didn't shove him. I put my hand on his shoulder. The guy was hectoring me to put more money in his pail. I said, 'You're not the only Santa Claus around' and he called me a cheapskate and a lot more and I said, 'Back off, fella,' and put my hand on his shoulder."

"I never should've told you about the story. Now I've gone and ruined your day. My bad. I am so so sorry."

Simon poured him a cup of coffee and put cream in it, too much cream, which he made a habit of. A bad habit, along with many others, including the self-accusations. A Midwestern habit. Simon tried to act like an English butler and say things like "Very good, sir" and "Brilliant" but he was from Sioux Center, Iowa, and his real name was Steve. He'd worked for the Sparrows for eleven years, ever since their marriage, and Mr. Sparrow wished he could fire him, but Mrs. Sparrow liked Simon. He was, after all, a cellist.

"Snowstorm in the Rockies," said Simon. "Thought you should know."

He put a newspaper down in front of James.

BLIZZARD DEATH TOLL STANDS AT TWO

A Butte, Montana, man died yesterday after he and his wife, 67, left home in their shirtsleeves to drive to the airport to fly to Tampa, not knowing the parking ramp was full and they would have to park in the overflow lot. The man, who also was 67, dropped his wife off at the terminal and parked the car and waited for the shuttle bus, which never came, due to scheduling problems. "Had Bernie walked briskly to the terminal and not waited around, he would still be alive today," said Sgt. Matt Hazzard of the airport police, who announced the victim's name as Bernie Rose. "We had thirteen wonderful years together and then God took him home," said Mrs. Rose from Tampa where she flew as scheduled. "Bernie was a man who embraced life and that's what I'm doing." Services will be held in the spring, she said, when the ground warms up.

Meanwhile, in Casper, Wyoming, a rancher suffering from cabin fever tried to thaw out his car with a shovelful of red-hot coals and the car caught fire. So he got out a toboggan and hitched up two steers to it and they pulled him for 4.2 miles down the road at high speed and then the two divided to go around a telephone pole where the man died of the impact. He was 47.

His name was Carl Koehler. Neighbors said he was quiet and kept to himself.

"Why are you showing me this?" said James. "Let's not start the day with a downer, okay?"

"Beg your pardon, sir. Thought you'd find it of interest. How is the new clock radio working out? Mrs. Sparrow said there was a problem."

5. He only wishes for a little pleasure — is that too much to ask?

Mrs. Sparrow had no appetite for breakfast. She had lost last night's dinner and taken a glass of Everwell Crystals to quell the uprising and now she needed to get her mind off it. She thought she would feel better if she took a brisk walk to the Art Institute and looked around in the French Impressionists section and visited the Matisse ballet dancers and Edward Hopper's nighttime diner with the lonely customers and the fry cook in white, which reminded her of Al's Breakfast Nook in Minneapolis where she spent an unhappy year going for her M.F.A. in creative writing where she learned that, despite the effusive praise of her instructors, she was not a writer. She was clever and facile and could spackle bright words on a page in the shape of a poem but she lacked heart. The fry cook in Al's had more heart about making a western omelet than she had for poetry. Breakfast was the high point of her day, the artist at the grill and the happy complaining of his clientele, and when she looked at the Hopper painting, she always cried. Sat on the bench fifteen feet away and wept until some kind soul asked if she was all right and she smiled up at him and said, "Never better." Which was true.

Mrs. Sparrow cried often and cried beautifully, and he had learned in eleven years of marriage that crying was part of her make-up and didn't indicate unhappiness and the worst thing he could say was, "What's wrong?" Nothing. She was clearing out her system, as simple as exhaling. She cried looking at certain paintings, and hearing *Madame Butterfly* and at Mimi's death in *La Bohème,* and at movies when the heroine is diagnosed with a deadly disease or the boy is ridiculed by his father or the lovers bid each other a chill farewell, and she wept at *A Christmas Carol* when Scrooge is guided by the Ghost to see the happiness of his early years and his love of the bountiful Belle, all of it destroyed by his sour passion for earning money. She loved those redemptive stories in which some cruel hard-hearted skeptic hates Christmas and then sees a bright star in the sky, or a candle in a window, or a child's face lit up in wonder, and his heart melts and he falls to his knees and repents.

"I wish you'd come see *A Christmas Carol* with me," she said. "The ghosts are wonderful this year. And Scrooge is electric."

"I saw it when I was a kid and found it terrifying. No need to repeat it."

She smiled at him sweetly. "I wish you enjoyed Christmas. Somehow I feel it's my fault. I haven't given you the Christmas you deserve."

"I might like Christmas more if it were in June," he said. "There's no good reason for it to be December 25th. There is no snow and ice in the Christmas story. The shepherds were out in the fields, for God's sake. Only reason they put it in December was to take over the old pagan holiday of Saturnalia and Christianize it, just like you'd buy up a theater and turn it into a church."

"It's the spirit of it that hits you so hard, darling. You're sentimental and you have to guard against it and that's why you put up that hard exterior. It's the sure sign of a soft heart."

Nice of her to think so, but not true. Not true. Christmas brought back powerful, painful memories of winter in Looseleaf, North Dakota. The little white house and the wind blowing and the ice on the windows and the side of his little fist melting the ice to make what looked like midget footprints. Tiny people walking barefoot on ice.

It was cold in the house. The African violets died and the cactus, some ferns survived and a funereal rubber plant. Daddy believed that if you couldn't see your breath when you talked, then the furnace was turned up too high, not that their family talked — they did not need to talk — they knew each other well enough without conversing, but they did respirate as they sat around the kitchen table under the Praying Hands plaque and ate their wieners and cheesy potatoes and clouds of steam came out of their mouths. It was like a prison camp. Any sort of playfulness or jokiness was discouraged. No reading at the table. Daddy talked. He said things like, "I don't know how I am going to make it through this week." And the statement sat there, a general lament at the state of things, and nobody said a word. The tyranny of complaint. It trumps everything else.

After supper Daddy listened to *Friendly Neighbors* on WLT as Mother washed the dishes and James curled up with his *World Almanac* which he'd read so many times he knew the major exports of all nations by heart, the state capitols and every member of the U.S. Senate and the top batters in the American and National leagues, but it was a ten-year-old almanac, Daddy refused to buy a new one, and some of the batters had retired. Bed-time was early. (What else was there to do?) Mother and Daddy slept in the downstairs bedroom in a double bed with deep grooves and James and Elaine and Benny slept in the cold attic on narrow hard beds and wore woolen long underwear to bed and there was no thought of bedwetting — it simply wasn't an option. They slept in the cold sheets and awoke with full bladders and pulled on layers of clothing — there was no lightweight thermal wear back then — you kept warm by the exertion of carrying heavy clothing: an eighty-pound child might wear thirty pounds of clothing, a little Sherpa going forth into the blizzard. It was a world of whiteness. Blazing white. It hurt your eyes. And school was never cancelled. Never. (Once you start canceling school, where do you draw the line?) So the children trudged through the blizzard to the road where the boys had made a snow fort and the girls huddled together and the boys peed in the snow as a defense against coyote and wolves and the girls crouched, shivering, whimpering, waiting for the bus to come and it was a long wait because the schoolbuses were frozen solid.

All of those memories — the grim mornings, the bowl of Hot Ralston cereal, the giant icicles, the frozen car — came back to him every December, and he felt *trapped* like a man in a deep cave, gripped by solid rock, and he felt a skittery panic though he was one of the richest men in Chicago. His heart fluttered at the first snowfall. Snow fell on the terrace on the 55th floor and though hot-water pipes embedded in the decking melted it, he felt constriction in his chest and as Christmas approached, he felt a sort of quiet terror.

It was due to a childhood trauma that he'd never told Mrs. Sparrow about. Which filled him with shame and self-loathing.

It was the Tongue On The Pump Handle Syndrome which he had tried to describe to his current shrink Dr. Boemer but he was from California and couldn't possibly understand.

His mother used to warn him about frostbite — *wear warm socks and mittens* — and she warned him to always breathe through his nose, not his mouth, so the air would be warmed before it reached the lungs — *you don't want to frost your lungs,* that was the phrase she used, "frost your lungs" — but the big thing she warned against was putting your tongue on a pump handle. Your tongue would freeze to it and there you'd be, stuck, and somebody would have to come and either warm up the handle with a blowtorch or else tear your tongue off it.

The tongue on the pump handle. Why did this loom so large in his mind? Pump handles were a rarity. He had never heard of an actual case of pump-handle-tongue freezing. Years later, after Daddy died, when Mother was opening up a little, he had asked her, "Why did you make such a big thing about not putting our tongues on pump handles?" and Mother said she had no idea what he was talking about and he said, "You warned me against putting my tongue on a pump handle because it would freeze to it and it's become a very big thing in my life." And his sister Elaine said he was being stupid. "Mother always was worried about you because you were sickly and difficult and didn't get along with other children," she said. "Someday they would have programs for special-needs kids like you but they didn't then. There was only your mom. And now you blame her for your weirdness?"

But the pump-handle obsession was stuck up there in his head. A sense of doom, a feeling that, one cold winter day, he would walk along and see a pump handle and be caught in its force field and stick his tongue to it and suffer horrible pain and his tongue would never recover. He would talk with a lisp afterward. No amount of speech therapy would help. And that was the basis of his horror of Christmas: the painful memory of a childhood fear that only grew stronger with the years. A fear of pump handles and also iron railings, iron poles, chains, clasps, shafts, masts, cast-iron pillars, pilasters, parapets, pipes, pegs, pins, pans, plates, panels, pommels, planks, pivots — once in a science museum in Poughkeepsie he stood enthralled by a pendulum, his tongue extended — knobs, rings, ribs, hoops, chucks, bolts, shells, spikes, sockets, shanks, tanks, trays, discs, hinges, hoods, hubcaps, gussets, cages, coils, cleats, caps, cups, couplings, capstans and davits, ductwork, trusses, bumpers, brackets, ratchets, switches, swivels, handles, spindles and sprockets, rockers, spacers, spools, screws, skirts, strips, stirrups, springs, manifolds — once, boarding a small plane in Pittsburgh he had felt powerfully drawn toward the propeller — hammers, housings, levers, louvers, vents, valves, bearings, beams, blades, clamps — once in Pomona he was photographed looking at an iron plinth and his tongue was hanging out. To strangers James was a big-shot and a tycoon and a handy target of abuse, but in fact he was a human being suffering from an obsession with iron and freezing weather and his tongue, clearly from a need for self-abasement and humiliation. Someday his dirty little secret would come out into the open . . .

CHI-TOWN TYCOON RESCUED BY FIREMEN, TONGUE FROZEN TO PUMP HANDLE; AT HOSPITAL, RECEIPTS FOUND IN POCKET LEAD TO CHARGE OF 14 COUNTS OF FRAUD; IF GUILTY, COULD FACE 150 YEARS IN JAIL

It was coming. If not this year, then next.

His only hope of escape?

Hawaii. It does not freeze in Hawaii. Not like you'd notice it.

6. The intractable problem of pump handles

He had tried yoga and the teacher Julie Ramanandra thought a position called the Blissful Rutabaga might be helpful. "Place the top of your head flat against the floor between your feet and then raise your legs very very high and straight in the air, keeping your hands in your pockets," she said. As she did this very thing. He got up and bowed and left the room.

A behavioral psychologist named Smucker told him to tie bells around his ankles so they jingled when he walked and to sing a calypso number,

"Mon, I Go To De Market Now An' Mak Much Mazuma." He said, "If you act happy, you will become happy. It actually works." James thanked him for the idea.

He went to an ill-tempered psychiatrist named Walters who dashed off a prescription for something called Mist On The Mountains and told him to take two right away and then one a day in the morning with food (but not with celery).

"What is this?" James said.

"Antidepressant."

"But which one?"

"What's the problem?"

"You can't tell me what it is?"

"What do you want? The chemical formula? A seminar on reuptake inhibitors? In a week you'll feel terrific. Have a nice day." The shrink went to the door and opened it.

"What does it do?" said James.

"What do you mean, 'what does it do?' It's an anti-depressant. It makes you happy. It induces amnesia and it snip-snip-snips the thread of memory and all those bad memories go drifting away like dirty bathwater and you'll be boyish and ebullient again."

"Will I still be able to read and write?"

"Probably."

"Probably!!!"

"There are trade-offs," said the psychiatrist. "But listen — you don't want it? Fine. I'll save it for somebody else. And *good luck.*" And presented a bill for $220 for consultation.

Pump Handle Syndrome. Ever since childhood, when the temperature dropped below twenty below, he got painful stomach cramps and nausea and felt listless lassitude and modern medicine couldn't do a thing for him, and then in Zurich once, at a party, he met a Nobel Prize–winning psycho-physiologist named Dr. Heinrich Hertz who had done interesting work in the field of polar obsessions at the *Zentral Kontor zie Ordnung Zuzammenschluss Medizinisch Forschung Verbindung Geschloss* and who put a blue slip of paper to Mr. Sparrow's tongue and examined it under a microscope and murmured to himself, *Gespruchen zee daskompenforshnittgennocktvairbruggendeehompen* and he told Mr. Sparrow he should move to a warm climate and avoid freezing weather — *Eis und Schnee — nicht! Nein!* — and he recommended spending winters in Hawaii and Mr. Sparrow bought Kuhikuhikapapa'u'maumau. And his pump-handle problem was solved.

Instant success! Exactly how modern science is supposed to work.

Problems that people used to struggle their whole lives with, pushing the boulder up the hill and then it overwhelms them and rolls back down and they have to push it back up — modern science can fix this with one wave of its beautiful hand. A little man with pince-nez glasses puts blue paper on your tongue (*Ahhhhh*) and looks up and says, "I vill tell you two tinks: you must komm in out of ze coldt! Undt you must shtay out of ze coldt!"

But he had to run a big corporation in Chicago, so he couldn't live full time at Kuhikuhikapapa'u'maumau and Mrs. Sparrow was active in the arts in Chicago and not ready to give up theater and dance and music and painting for a life of collecting seashells and making necklaces of hibiscus blossoms so Mr. Sparrow stayed Chicago-bound. Meanwhile his pump-handle problem only got worse. In cold weather, he had to force himself to keep his tongue in his mouth and not put it on car door handles or the bronze busts of Studs Terkel and Ernie Banks outside the library or the railing going up the front stairs of the Bunyan Club.

Dr. Boemer told him that he was exhibiting obsessive-compulsive behavior and that there was a medical device that might help him, but then Dr. Boemer got to talking about other OCD cases he'd seen — obsessive hand-wringing, obsessive counting of ceiling tiles, obsessive ironing and pacing and talking, obsessive Facebook updating and friending, a male patient who went to a gym three times a day to shoot free-throws, exactly three hundred each time, and how Dr. Boemer had gotten him down to one hundred. Dr. Boemer was fascinated by OCD and he told about case after case. Obsessive-compulsive piano practicing. Guitar tuning. Making of lists. Clipping articles from newspapers and filing them. Nose picking. E-mailing jokes. One of his patients obsessively brushed her teeth down to tiny stumps. Another made bomb threats, hundreds a day, but always honking an ooga-ooga horn so they'd know it wasn't for real.

Dr. Boemer went on and on, his voice

like a cold engine trying to start. The hour was up and Mr. Sparrow was standing with his hand on the doorknob and Dr. Boemer could not stop telling about yet one more interesting OCD case. Being from California, frozen pump handles had no reality for him, but obsessive treadmill running did, and obsessive copyediting and grammar correcting, solitaire playing, throat clearing, belly itching, Web surfing, folk dancing, digital photographing, pants adjusting, geyser gazing, apologizing. He had a client named Mrs. Sanderson who could not speak a simple sentence without prefacing it with a "I'm so sorry but —" or "Begging your pardon —." Mr. Sparrow said, "Excuse me but I'm fairly certain that it's a violation of medical ethics to disclose these details," and Dr. Boemer went on telling about OCDs he had known, as Mr. Sparrow left the office and stood at the elevator ("There was this one guy I recall who hummed to himself. Boy that was a case. We worked on him for almost two years.") and the elevator doors closed and Mr. Sparrow never went back. But the tongue-on-the-pump-handle fear remained strong.

Except if he went to Kuhikuhikapapa'u'maumau.

7. An old argument rears its sweet little head once again

He stood under the hot shower listening to Bach's *Brandenburg Concerto No. 6* and, without thinking, pressed his tongue against a pipe, which was hot, and he recoiled and slipped slightly and joggled something in his lower back. *Call Nicole the shiatsu therapist,* he thought. He put on a pair of chinos and a white shirt and sandals and slipped into the kitchen where Simon had the breakfast made, two poached eggs (slightly runny) on rye toast, OJ, a latte, a sliced pear.

"Have you decided what time you

wish to leave, sir?" Simon said. "All is in high readiness on all fronts. The troops are at attention, awaiting your command. The plane is fueled, the pilots rested, the snacks replenished —"

"I know, I know. First I have to find out when Mrs. Sparrow wants to go and then we're all set."

Joyce returned from her walk at 10:44 A.M. and said it was brisk and bracing outdoors and good for her ailment. She took off her wire-rim glasses and stood across the table and he was struck with a rush of dumb love for her. The great question of his life (Who do you love?) resolved in this tall broad-shouldered woman with mahogany hair tied back in a copper clip, grinning at him, crinkling her Roman nose, in her cowboy shirt and gray sweatpants, the sheer elegance of her, and he stood up and put his arms around her, tears in his eyes.

He met her the same year Coyote Corp. got off the ground when he judged a Christmas Gift-Wrap Contest at Marshall Field, which she won in the final round, the globular round, wrapping a basketball in golden paper, and hers had not a wrinkle or crinkle or rip in it. And he sat next to her at the awards luncheon and she talked about her aspirations in theater and he about coyote grass and he proposed a weekend at Mackinac Island and she told him that she would feel terrible guilt about such a thing because during her acting-school days in New York she had, in order to protect her cheap sublet of an apartment on West 86th and Broadway, dressed up in a black silk dress and a mantilla and attended early morning mass, impersonating the old lady from whom she'd sublet and who had died, and after eight months in the role of Mrs. Manicotti she came to feel a true religious devotion she had not felt in her upbringing as a Methodist in Wauwatosa, which caused a rift with her family who were willing to accept agnosticism but Catholicism was another matter. "Whatever we are, we are not Catholic," said her mother. "We stand. We do not kneel." But Joyce loved the kneeling part especially at midnight mass on Christmas Eve, when her faith was renewed, if only for a few days, and so she was not sure she could make love with him at Mackinac Island, but by the time she had told him the whole long story, they were in his apartment on a couch in front of a gas fireplace and unwrapping each other and they made tender and languorous love and fell asleep in each other's arms and from that perfect night came eleven years of pleasant marriage, except for the Christmas holidays, of which this one was shaping up (he thought) to be the worst.

"Oh darling, I love you so much and I love our beautiful apartment and it is such a busy time of year, what with *Hansel and Gretel* at the Lyric and *A Child's Christmas In Wales* and the Bach *Christmas Oratorio* and I just wonder if we couldn't stay right here for Christmas. I could put on a muu-muu and make you a puu-puu platter with fresh pineapple and turn the heat up and play Hawaiian music and save on using all that aviation fuel that is so hard on the ozone layer and maybe invite some needy person such as your sister Elaine in Fort Wayne to come and share the bounty with us."

"Darling," said James. "You and I have always had such wonderful times in Kuhikuhikapapa'u'maumau. And an overheated apartment in Chicago is no equivalent. And Elaine is a mess. Let's not spend the holiday doing intervention therapy."

"We had beautiful times there," she said. "I'll remember them always. But this virus has affected me in strange ways and I feel a need to stay in the city and be with friends here. I don't know anybody in Kuhikuhikapapa'u'maumau."

"We could bring your friends with us. The plane can carry eight."

"Oh darling — my friends have jobs. They can't just pick up for a couple weeks and go to Hawaii. What's wrong with Chicago, sweetie?"

He thought, *Maybe I need to tell her about the pump handle thing. What a huge thing it's become in my life.*

On the other hand, she might say, "Why didn't you tell me that a long time ago?"

"I will do anything if you'll come to Kuhikuhikapapa'u'maumau."

She smiled. "Anything?"

"Anything. You name it."

"Will you have a baby with me?"

Oh dear. The old subject that had come up so often in the past six years. The Mommy Moment.

He did not know anybody with children who was as happy as he was and that was the plain truth. Children meant the death of romance. The end of freedom, the beginning of indentured servitude. The stink, the noise, the sheer *immaturity* of children. Mrs. Sparrow wanted a baby and Mr. Sparrow wanted a good life.

He said, "Maybe you're right. Maybe Kuhikuhikapapa'u'maumau isn't the greatest idea. We can do Christmas in Chicago if you like. Go to shows and stuff."

"Kuhikuhikapapa'u'maumau is paradise. Sometimes I dream that I'm sleeping there with you and the windows are open and the white curtains are rippling and I can hear the surf. And then I get out of bed and there's a baby in a crib, a baby with dark hair like mine and ocean breezes blowing over her."

Let's you and I spend Christmas out

there. We can talk about children when we get there. Let's pack a bag and call up the plane and go. It was a bad day the other day. So what? Everybody has a bad day. Forget it. We belong together. That's what he wanted to say. *We had some great Christmases out there. Remember? We're good together.*

She was giving him her intense loving look. "It's Christmas. I wish we had a child to share it with."

"I know you do."

"I woke up last night and started crying, just thinking about it."

"I'm sorry."

"I'll be okay."

"Of course you will. It's just that time of month."

She shot him a sharp look. "It's not about that at all. Believe me."

"So what should we tell all the employees waiting for us at Kuhikuhikapapa'u'maumau?"

"The people at Kuhikuhikapapa'u'maumau would be overjoyed if we had a baby."

The Baby Problem came up the week before during the PMS argument about Mrs. Sparrow's mother Marge who lived in Wauwatosa and called her daughter twice a day and with Christmas coming on she was good and weepy and remembering her late husband Mutt and how he loved his outdoor Christmas lights. He put them up around Halloween. Zipper lights, Santa dancing a hula with Frosty, Rudolph leading the Wise Men. A sign on the roof flashing *Ha!* and then *le* and *lu* and *yeah*. Marge sat in her kitchen in the dark, the lights flashing outside, and drank a little Bailey's Irish Cream and wept for the old days.

Fine. James liked Marge okay.

He assumed it was PMS. It had a PMSsy feel to it. PMS hit Joyce harder than it did most women. She lay in the dark weeping and listening to music and in the throes of hormone poisoning, she worked herself up into a state and thought (or thought she thought) that James thought her mother's Christmas lights were stupid and garish. He had no such opinion! He had been careful not to form an opinion. The lights simply were what they were. He knew that in times of deep toxic PMS, he should show endless patience and kindness, and that particular night she emerged red-eyed from her office and said, "I've decided that we don't need to invite my mother here for the holidays. She's weird and depressing and you get depressed enough by Christmas without my mother adding to the problem." He knew he should have said: *I love your mother and I enjoy seeing her — at Christmas or any other time. She is a dear and good woman. Let's not talk about it now, darling. Let's go to bed and I'll hold you in my arms and kiss your neck.*

What he actually said was, "If that's what you'd like, fine. Maybe she has other plans."

She said, "Well, that's what you'd like, isn't it?"

"If that's what you want, darling," he said.

She said, "I remember how irritated

you got with her last year when she talked about how she couldn't understand people objecting to Christmas trees in schools. You sat there, grinding your teeth."

"I didn't grind my teeth, I simply disagreed with her on constitutional grounds."

"She has gone through so much and now she has her gluten problem . . ."

"I know —"

"To live your life knowing that if you should sit down next to someone who baked that morning, your throat will swell up and you have to find the emergency kit and before you can find it, maybe you're on the floor, clutching at your throat and making strangled animal sounds and people are stepping around you and averting their eyes —"

"Darling, invite your mother here if you want her to come."

And she broke down sobbing that she didn't want her mother to come where she wasn't wanted. He tried to reason with her. She said that she was not about to throw away her flesh and blood as if they were garbage. "My mother is seventy-eight, and I'm supposed to — what? throw her in the ditch? Because she's an inconvenience? She's my mom. And someday she's not going to be there anymore and I'm gonna miss her so much. And I'm going to feel terrible that I never gave her a grandchild." She blew her nose, *Breaughhhh.* "Oh James, is that why you refuse to give me a baby? The fear of heredity? That a baby would look like my mother?"

And she ran sobbing into the bedroom and locked herself in the bathroom and when he tapped on the door and begged her to come out, she said she needed to be alone right now. And she emerged an hour later in her white bathrobe and apologized in a chill tone of voice and took a sleeping pill and went to sleep at 9 o'clock. It sort of put a damper on the week. But now that was over and they'd moved on, he thought, to post-PMS, and he was ready to go. The plane was ready. The bags were packed and lined up by the service elevator. The staff at Kuhikuhikapapa'u'maumau was awaiting their arrival. The sun was shining there. The mangoes and pineapple were picked. *They should have been happy!*

Somewhere down the hall he heard the song —

Do you hear what I hear?
A song, a song, very unappealing,
Leaking like asbestos from the ceil-
ing.

And then someone switched it off.

He wanted to tell her, *This pump handle obsession has got me by the throat, babes. I am dying inside. I'd be sunk without you. Whether I were in Chicago or Kuhikuhikapapa'u'maumau.* But he was afraid of losing her. If she knew how bunged-up he was and crippled by dread and shame, maybe she'd decide he wasn't worth sticking around for. Dump him and get a nice divorce settlement and be a matron of the arts.

8. A phone call from the past

His phone rang. It was his cousin Liz in Looseleaf. "Do you have a minute?" she said.

"What is it?"

"You're in a rush. I can hear it. Listen, I'll send you a text message."

"Just tell me what's wrong."

"It's nothing important so don't get all het up."

"About what?"

"Listen — Jimmy, I can tell I've upset you. I'll call back when you settle down."

"What's going on?"

"So you didn't hear about Daddy?"

"What about Uncle Earl?"

"I shouldn't even say. He didn't want you to know."

"Know what?"

"It's nothing. He's old. Everything comes to an end. There are no guarantees. We'll deal with it. You've got enough to worry about."

"Tell me what's going on, Liz."

"I shouldn't have said anything. He had to go into the hospital on Tuesday."

"What's wrong?"

"Daddy told me not to call you because he knew you'd be upset. I'm sorry I opened my big mouth."

James took the phone in his right hand and whacked the table with it four, five, six times, and then said, "Liz, if you don't stop beating around the bush, I'm going to fly up there and give you a Dutch rub. Remember the Dutch rub, Liz? It stings. I can make you cry."

Mrs. Sparrow got up from the table and whispered, "I have to go throw up now."

"What's wrong?" he said.

"Are you sitting down?" said Liz.

"It's my stomach flu," said Mrs. Sparrow.

"I think you should consult a doctor," he said.

"He already did," said Liz. "Three of them."

The thought of pump handles crossed his mind. Maybe Uncle Earl had wandered out in a daze and put his tongue on frozen iron and then yanked and the whole organ had been uprooted and he lay there bleeding, the snow around his head turning bright red, until a newsboy found him and now he was in a coma.

"His left eyeball fell out," said Liz.

"His eyeball fell out????"

Mrs. Sparrow put her hand to her mouth and gagged.

"It was only the left one. He was watching the Lawrence Welk Christmas special on TV and Bobby and Betty did a beautiful tap dance to 'O Holy Night' and Daddy got weepy and rubbed his eye and it just fell out. It was hanging by the optic. He has skin cancer and it spread to his eyes. But they popped it right back in. He's fine. No problem. He didn't want me to call you and bother you."

"Oh my god."

"Anyway, could you call him and cheer him up a little? You know he thinks the sun rises and sets on you, and he still talks about the time you flew out here for his birthday — when was that? Ten years ago? Anyway, you mean the world to him, and frankly — I shouldn't say this, but . . . I don't know as he'll make it to Christmas." And then she broke down and cried and hung up. Not like Liz to fall apart like that, she being a member of the National Rifle Association and all.

And he called Buzz at the plane and said, "I've gotta fly up to Looseleaf. It's not far from Bismarck. They built that regional airport there."

He turned to Mrs. Sparrow. "My uncle Earl is dying. He has skin cancer and his left eyeball fell out. They think it's in the last stage."

"The happy uncle? The one who always made you laugh when you were growing up?"

"Yes. I'm flying up there today. I wish you'd come but I suppose you can't."

The question hung in the air — *Would you come with me?* — but then she felt very ill and headed for the bathroom. She came back a few minutes later looking wan and depleted. She was sorry. She would come to Hawaii if she could, it all depended on how she felt, and right now she felt like death on toast.

9. Why he must change plans and fly to Looseleaf

Uncle Earl was the brightest penny in a handful of loose change. He was the happiest man in Looseleaf, who every day did all he could to put a sunny smile on the gloomy faces around him. He loved electricity. He was the superintendent of the county hydroelectric station, a spotless brick building alongside the Stanley River, and he believed in hydroelectric as God's gift to man and the cheapest and most reliable source of power and if somebody's lights went out in the middle of the night, Earl climbed into the truck and went off cheerfully to repair the problem. He was a fixer-upper and a friend to all and he was James's salvation as a boy growing up in a desolate dusty town in an eternity of wheat and soybeans. He took James fishing summer mornings early when the mists hung over the water of Lake Winnesissebigosh and recited Poe and Longfellow and Edgar Guest.

He was a cheerful optimist in a family of cranks and grumblers and mournful men and sour women with hounddog faces all aggrieved about money and cars and worried about kids poking their eyes out with sharp sticks and having to learn Braille and go around with a dog on a leash or the baby eating fistfuls of toilet bowl cleanser, or communists taking over, or a small plane crashing into the house, or the Christmas decorations strung above Main Street coming loose in a wind and fifty-pound angels falling down and killing someone. And of course the danger of Christmas tree fires. And there in this sinkhole of anxiety stood Uncle Earl, smiling, bowtied, neat moustache, hair parted in the middle, and a carnation in his lapel, and if a priest walked by, or a blond, or someone from Minnesota, Earl had a joke for you, or two if you showed interest — and fresh ones, not the tired old jokes you'd heard before. Out of sheer good will, he was apt to break into "Kathleen Mavourneen" or "Five Foot Two, Eyes of Blue, Has Anybody Seen My Gal." He carried ginger snaps with him that had a real snap to them because ginger stimulates clear thinking. He'd make ginger ale punch and put on a record of the Mormon Tabernacle Choir singing:

By the old Moulmein Pagoda
looking eastward to the sea,
There's a Burma girl a-settin'
and I know she thinks of me.
For the wind is in the palm trees,
And the temple bells they say,
"Come you back, you British soldier,
come you back to Mandalay."

And the man and the boy stood and marched in time to the chorus, swinging their arms, and sang at the tops of their voices:

On the road to Mandalay,
Where the flying fishes play,

And the dawn comes up like thunder
Out of China cross the bay.

Earl had no enemies and held no grudges and when a new county board was elected in 1953 on a platform of fighting Communist infiltration and decided to abandon hydroelectric for a giant diesel generator and took trips to New Orleans, Dallas, Las Vegas, and Phoenix to search for the proper generator, and in Tucson met a diesel salesman who took them out to a fine steakhouse and introduced them to three young women named Tammy, Bambi, and Trixie, and the next morning the board signed the contract, and the diesel was shipped to Looseleaf, the hydroelectric plant was shut down, and the diesel got hooked up and ran, more or less, for a couple of years, and the price of electrical power tripled, and Uncle Earl was fired and replaced by the brother-in-law of an anti-communist, that didn't darken Earl's nature at all. He just opened a vegetable stand and sold watermelon, sweet corn, peppers, tomatoes, potatoes, and Swiss chard. And he told James, "Don't worry about the past and don't try to solve the future. Bravery and adventure! That's the ticket! Don't sit and gather moss. Get up, get out, do what you dream of doing, and if it doesn't work, it doesn't work, and you don't need to make that particular mistake again, but at least you won't get old wondering what if you had."

Like the Christmas Uncle Earl decided to experiment with candles on the Christmas tree. He had seen this in Victorian picture books, the master of the house lighting the candles and the children dazed with wonder, and so he went ahead — secretly, of course — why spoil the surprise? — and bought an 8-foot Norwegian pine and six dozen clip-on candleholders and let Aunt Myrna hang the bulbs and doodads and gewgaws and tinsel and on Christmas Eve he snuck out of the Methodist church during the singing of "Silent Night" and trotted home and hung the candles and then, when he glimpsed Myrna and the children and the Sparrow family and Aunt Mona and Boo and Sherm heading for the house for the oyster stew and the cardamom buns, he took a little gas torch and lit 72 candles just in time for the whole gang to come piling in the front door, but they made a beeline for the kitchen, not the living room where the astonishing thing stood in its flaming glory, and when he cried, "Let's all go in the living room!" nobody budged. So he cried out, "Let's open presents!" But Myrna was already handing out cups of mulled wine. So, in desperation, and as a sort of joke, he yelled, "The tree's on fire!" And the whole bunch mobbed into the living room and indeed it was and James's mother, who got there first, fainted at the sight and landed on little Liz and broke her collarbone and she had to be driven forty miles to a hospital, which cast a shadow on the evening. Aunt Myrna said to him, "How could you have done such a thing and not have warned me?" but it was Earl's way to do things impulsively, with great enthusiasm. And thereby made a vivid Christmas memory for each and all and on succeeding Christmases the mere sight of a cluster of candles brought it all back, the majesty and the terror of it.

10. He descends through the storm into the land of dark memories

He got to Midway at two in the afternoon and the *Lucky Lady* was pulled up in front of the V.I.P. terminal and Buzz was waiting to take the bags from Ramon and stow them in the tail. Buzz had put on his lucky white silk scarf and his leather helmet. The snow was coming down hard. He followed Buzz to the plane and Buzz asked where Mrs. Sparrow was. "She'll fly commercial on Christmas Day," he said. "She's feeling under the weather."

"We could come back here and pick

her up."

"We could do that. We'll see."

Buddy had the coffee made and a basket of fresh croissants and raspberry jam and all the newspapers, which Mr. Sparrow stuffed under his seat. He buckled himself in and looked out the window at a little Cessna wheeling off toward the runway. No interest in newspapers today — he was afraid of what he might find out. The company was wallowing in this recession and his radio stations were tanking — *why had he ever wanted to get into radio? Dumb dumb dumb* — and the Lake Superior Cruise Line was a loser — *who wants to sail the coast of Wisconsin?* — and the publishing division came out with a magazine called *Sleepers* aimed at people with sleep issues and strong literary interests. Not a success. And in November came that nasty article in the *Mid-Atlantic Journal of Medicine,* a little study jiggered by a disgruntled nobody in a lab coat purporting to show that coyote grass is somehow tied (it isn't) to a loss of language skills. Sales of 4xPrime went in the toilet. Mr. Sparrow's marketing people met behind closed doors and anguished over the thing and meanwhile the story spread.

When it comes to the rich, people are anxious to believe the absolute worst!

And so this morning he had no idea, none, how much he actually was worth, $230 million or $150 million or $80 million, only that cuts needed to be made, sails trimmed, which led to an unfortunate story in the paper

(*Tycoon Reneges On Promise To Boys*), which was picked up by the local TV news ("Faced with major financial losses, Mr. Sparrow opted to back out of a $5 million commitment to the Boys' Club rather than sell his luxury vacation home on Hawaii, or his private jet" — there, film footage of the interior of the *Lucky Lady,* the wide-ride leather seats, the buffet laid out on a table, and him asleep, head lolling back, mouth open, glasses askew, thirty pounds overweight (*WHERE DID THIS PICTURE COME FROM????* some embittered employee?), the plane pitched forward into its descent and entered a gray cloud bank and went down, down, down, without a break in the clouds. Deeper and deeper it went, like a cage descending into a mine shaft, the cloud getting darker and thicker. And as he looked out the window into the murk, the memory of that old Christmas of the Great Flu came back to him. His humiliation in the snow. And the laughter from the neighbors' next door — their old pump behind the garage, the handle loose, shaking in the wind, making a sort of low guttural chuckle.

As the *Lucky Lady* descended, Mrs. Sparrow called him to say she felt better but rather heavy and logy. "Maybe you should go on to Hawaii without me," she said. He told her that he couldn't possibly think of such a thing but in fact he already had thought of it once or twice. "Please," she said. "I'm perfectly fine. I want you to go. I'll come next week."

"Well, I might do that," he said. "We'll see." Meaning that he'd fly to

Hawaii that night.

The plane bucketed in the clouds and he felt a heaviness in his gut and then the plane broke through a low ceiling — a few hundred feet — and down over snowy fields, a farmyard with six big blue silos, a windbreak row of poplars, a stretch of corn stubble, a county road with no traffic moving, and then down on the tarmac. Buzz put the brakes on hard and reversed the engines and they stopped in short order and turned sharply in toward the terminal where he could see, through the falling snow, a few figures in parkas waiting beside a pickup truck, its hazard lights flashing.

The Looseleaf Regional Air Facility had been built with federal money back in the Reagan years on the theory that big shots, if they could fly in on their private jets, might build a factory there, a distribution center, a phone center, a warehouse, *something,* to provide jobs to keep young people from blowing away to Minneapolis and Chicago. The Upper Missouri Progress Coalition (UMPH) had gotten the airport built but not many big execs flew in, and not much materialized — a grommet plant that employed 14, the Taxidermy Hall of Fame, his own coyote grass factory (20 employees, mostly seasonal), and that was about the extent of it.

The plane wheeled around to the terminal, bumping over the little drifts. A kid in blue coveralls came running out with the chocks and one of the parkas turned out to be Mr. Sparrow's cousin-in-law Leo Wimmer. With the furry hood around his face, and the snow falling, he looked like a last survivor of the Shackleton expedition. He stuck his head in the open door and said, "Wow. Nice. This is the way to travel, I guess." Married to cousin Liz, a second marriage for both of them, undertaken on a weekend trip to a gun convention in Mandan. Leo had a rather blunt personality so everyone assumed alcohol was involved in the romance, but Liz was a ferocious Republican and so maybe it all balanced out.

Buzz peered out the door and looked up at the sky and said, "This ain't going to be passable for long, Mr. Sparrow. Forecast says there's a foot or more of snow on the way. My recommendation is that you zip into town and zip back and let's get airborne in twenty minutes."

James put on his black wool coat and his fur cap. “Long time no see,” said Leo. “Liz would’ve come but she had a little crisis. She came home from having four wisdom teeth pulled and was zonked on Vicodin and went upstairs to use the toilet and she pulled about a hundred yards of toilet paper off the roll so the toilet overflowed and it was leaking through the dining room chandelier and dripping from the crystal beads and I can’t get up on a ladder because my prostate is the size of a seedless orange and I’m due to go in for a ream job after the first of the year, so I left your cousin mopping up pee off the good rug and I go out to shovel out the car and I get hit by a snowmobile. Isn’t that just the way it is?” And he clapped James on the back. “It’s good to see you.”

"I'm in something of a rush, Leo. Just came to say hi to Uncle Earl. I hear he's at death's door."

"Well, some days he is and others he isn't. I mean, everybody in North Dakota is at death's door if you want to look at it that way. But for many of us, the door is locked. If you get my drift."

James tried to get Leo moving but the ground crew was gathered around, three men who'd never met a man with a private plane, evidently. Leo suggested a picture. His camera was in his car.

"How about we run into town first, Leo? I don't have much time."

"Hey, it'll only take a minute." But it took sixteen minutes. His car was parked on the other side of the building. He had to search his various pockets to find the keys. The car door was frozen shut since he'd had it washed that morning. They had to find a hairdryer to thaw it out and that took a while. James stood by Leo's station wagon, shifting his weight from foot to foot, clapping his gloves together, clearing his throat, pacing, trying to move things along with a show of restlessness. Snow was drifting around the *Lucky Lady*. "How about one of you guys get out a plow and make a sweep of the runway?" said Buzz. The ground crew discussed that for a couple minutes, whether plowing now would do any good or just make the pavement slicker. They decided to wait and see. This was the pace of life in Looseleaf. People didn't jump to a task, ever. Every problem needed to be looked at from all angles, opinions sought, mulled over.

The terminal was a hollow shell of peeling paint and unfinished concrete — two empty ticket counters and a baggage carousel, never used, and a little office in the corner where the ground crew hung out. The smell of burnt coffee in the air, a stack of empty pizza boxes. He called Uncle Earl from the terminal office who sounded pretty chipper for a dying man. "Remember that time the snowbanks were fifteen feet high and you and me had to shovel and throw the snow way up and our arms got tired?" said Uncle Earl. "And we tied clotheslines to our belts so if there was an avalanche they could pull us out in time? Remember that?"

"I thought you were sick, Uncle Earl."

"Ha! Some people wish I were! Not sick, just feeling a chill. I crawled into my nest here, piled up some quilts and burrowed down like an old rat and was living on peanut butter cookies and water chestnuts, but now that you're here, I'm fine. When you coming over? Faye's tickled to death, she can't wait to see you."

His cousin Faye was the one he was hoping not to see, recently moved back to Looseleaf after her husband Floyd kicked the bucket in Sedona, Arizona. She was a poet, a painter, and a professional storyteller. She hired herself out to public schools and went around in a beady dress and a feathery hat and told ancient Ojibway myths such as "How The Coyote Got His Name" and "Where The Snow Goes In Summer," though she was no more Ojibway than the Pope in Rome.

"I was going to come by to see you," James said. "But if you're busy, I can come back after New Year's."

"Not up to a thing. Waiting for spring. Waiting to hear the bluebirds sing."

"Let me take care of a few things first."

"You take your time. I am going nowhere whatsoever."

11. Into the storm he goes with only minutes to spare before the airport closes

Snow was falling and blowing sideways as Leo drove him into Looseleaf at 5 m.p.h. and he could barely make out the red light on the water tower, the grain elevator by the train tracks, the old high school and the bell tower of St. Margaret's Catholic church. A grim-voiced announcer on the radio said that people should drive only if necessary and avoid the back roads.

"If you get stuck or run off the road, turn on your hazard lights and hang a red flag from your radio antenna. Do not set out on foot. Remain in your vehicle. Conserve body heat by hugging each other. If this is not possible, use floor mats for insulation."

"This'll all blow over in an hour. I don't know what the big panic's all about," said Leo. "They've got a plow, the boys'll get that runway clear in fifteen minutes."

Leo had a habit of slowing down and speeding up in a nervous rhythmic way. He reached for the radio dial — "Don't turn it off," said James. "I need to know the weather."

The announcer was saying, "If you are stranded in a deserted area, stay with your car. When the wind lets up, spell out the word H E L P in the snow and put rocks or tree limbs in the letters to attract the attention of rescue airplanes. Beware of hypothermia and frostbite. Breathe cold air through your nose, not your mouth, so as not to frost your lungs. And when you are around pump handles, railings, or other iron objects outdoors, do not put your tongue on them or your tongue will freeze to the object and rescuers may not be able to hear your muffled cries for help until it is too late."

"Pump handles!" cried Leo. "How ridiculous! Who's going to put their tongue on a pump handle?"

"Kids might. You never know. They're dangerous, I know that."

And then came the meaty voice of the Governor saying that everything that could be done was being done and that he was monitoring the situation closely along with federal officials and people should stay in their homes and remain calm.

Go back to the plane, go back to the plane. He thought they were heading for Uncle Earl's house but then Leo turned left on Fillmore. "Where we going?" James cried. Leo said, "I promised Liz you'd come say hi."

"Leo, I've got to get out of here today —"

"Don't worry, we'll get you out."

"We're looking at a very small window here."

"Where you got to get out to?"

He was about to say "Hawaii" and then thought better of it. A man headed for Hawaii might not get the cooperation from a North Dakotan that he was hoping for. He said, "I'm on a secret mission, Leo — I wish I could tell you more but I'm working for the C.I.A. and I'm dropping provisions to a patrol that's probing the border into Saskatchewan. Canadian Intelligence — CanTell — is slipping some of their boys across and we need to find out why."

"Dangerous?"

"The Canucks play for keeps, Leo. Some of our guys have driven into automatic car washes and never got out alive. Those big rollers busted the windows and they were waxed to death. Lots at stake. The whole border west of Detroit is pretty much in play. Parts of it never were marked clearly. You've got iridium deposits up there, mica, quartz, oilfields — and the combination of quartz and oil is extremely significant."

The snow was coming down harder. And then Leo slammed on the brakes and they skidded to the left and just missed Jack Cobb crossing the street and James cranked down the window. "Sorry!" he said.

"Jimbo! Boy O boy. I shoulda let you guys run me down, I coulda collected a million bucks for mental anguish! Ha ha ha ha ha ha ha!" Jack reached in and shook his hand. His breath smelled of cheese and coffee, dead muskrats, and rotten lumber. "What's new with you, Jimbo?"

"Trying to get out of town."

"Thought you left a long time ago."

Mr. Cobb laughed. It reminded him, he said, of a joke about the small town so small that — what? How did it go?

"The small town where the population stays the same because every time a baby is born, a man has to leave town," said James.

No, that wasn't the one. But this

joke was about having babies.

"The one about the man and his wife who had twelve kids because they lived near the train tracks and when the midnight train came through and woke him up, he'd say, 'Well, should we go back to sleep or what?' and she'd say, 'What —' "

No, but it was about sex.

"I've got to run, Jack. Really. Got to catch a plane."

"Aw, nothing's flying in this weather, Jimbo. Come in and have a beer. It's been years."

Jack was opening the van door now. "Let's have a look at you, for cripes' sake." He saw the black wool coat and let out a low whistle. "Nice coat. How much that set you back, Jimbo?" James had to wrestle the door from him and pull it shut and lock it and even then Jack pounded on the glass. "Think you're hot stuff? Well, you're not. I wouldn't piss on you if you were on fire!"

"Immaturity knows no age limit," said Leo. By now the snow was coming down thick, big fluffy flakes like chicken feathers, and now Leo couldn't figure out which way was west. He turned left onto a street that didn't feel like the right way but James didn't say anything because the street was so familiar, and then it dawned on him — His street! His old street. Davis Avenue. And his boyhood home was up ahead on the right. The little white story-and-a-half frame house with the two oaks in the front yard.

He used to walk down that driveway to school and turn right to take the long way around and avoid the

Durbins who lived between his house and school and who were laying for him. He used to shoot baskets in that driveway, back before the garage was brought down by carpenter ants. Come December and the Arctic blast, their old Ford coupe sat out in the open and froze to the gravel. Daddy put the key in the ignition and it was like trying to start a box of hammers. So he brought out a bucket of hot coals and put them under the engine block to warm up the crankcase oil to where it'd move and then James had to get behind the wheel while Daddy pushed it down the slight incline of the driveway and at just the exact right moment, James had to pop the clutch and if he timed it exactly right the momentum of the car turned over the engine and it fired up, and if he didn't do it right, the car jerked to a stop and Daddy had to call up Mr. Wick to come over with jumper cables and to be beholden to Mr. Wick was something Daddy preferred to avoid. Mr. Wick was a Democrat and an agnostic, or the next thing to it.

He told Leo to slow down as they came to his old house and Leo stopped. There was a new garage plus a deck where the old incinerator used to be, where he used to burn the trash including aerosol cans that said, "Danger: May Explode If Exposed to Open Flame." And the driveway where the old Ford coupe rolled slowly, creaking, little James hanging onto the wheel and peering out through a tiny aperture in the frost on the windshield, the car jolting over the bumps, bouncing like a wild bronco, the shock absorbers frozen solid, the boy hanging on to the wheel, his foot slipping off the gas pedal as Daddy cried, "Now! Now!" and trees flying past while the boy hung on and then he popped the clutch and the engine roared and the car jumped forward and he slammed on the brake and remembered to hit the clutch too and the old Ford sat there, shaking, and Daddy opened the door and said, "Get out before you kill it."

And off he trudged to the bus stop, feet crunching on the snow, the sound of sharp cracks that might be trees cracking or maybe the earth itself. A planet with hot molten rock in the middle, that is frozen solid at the top — something has to give. The earth cracks wide open and limbs fall off trees and pin you to the ground. Or maybe you walk across the snow and step into a bear trap. *Whack!* it breaks your leg. Or you step into a deep hole, and there's a bear in it, a bear who has eaten nothing but dirt and leaves for weeks and is very hungry. Winter was a world of anxiety for young James. Bears, bear traps, trees falling, and then there was the fear of Communists. They could come skiing down from Canada, across an undefended border, and line the children up in the playground and give them a choice: either say "I hate America and I don't believe in God whatsoever" or else put your tongue on a frozen pump handle. What would he do then? He knew what he'd do, he'd renounce America and God and the Communists would all clap and cheer but God wouldn't like it and in the next instant the boy would be in hell, flames licking at his feet, burning people walking by.

"What are you so quiet about?" said Leo.

"It's not the right road," he said.

"It's not?"

It was not the right road. It was the road that went past the road to the airport and by the time they figured that out, James had come to the sad realization that he was not going to fly to Kuhikuhikapapa'u'maumau to-night. It wasn't going to happen.

He told Leo to stop and he got out of the car and stood in the street, in the hush of snowfall. Nobody was out shoveling, everybody was sitting tight. The electric carillon at the Methodist church was playing "O Come, O Come, Emmanuel" where the sermon on Sunday, according to the marquee, would be "Behold Him, O Ye Peoples." Whiteness glittering everywhere, the wind whipping up little eddies of snow on the drifts across the frozen tundra. The old house on the corner was Daryl Holmberg's and there was old Daryl in the living room, blue TV light flickering on his sleepy face, his old classmate, a Methodist deacon now but back then he liked to torture smaller nerdier boys and throw jagged iceballs at people. James's dad's friend Archie Pease, who lived across the street wrote a column for the *Weekly Binder* ("Pease Porridge"), and next door was Rochelle Westendorp, the town librarian, who was mad at James for being so rich and not giving much to the library. And Paul Werberger,

a bachelor who lived with four dogs and six cats and collected old magazines and played the banjo. And then his Aunt Mona's house was up ahead, a little cottage under a giant Norway pine, where she lived until Gene passed away and then she fled North Dakota for Ventura, California, and never was forgiven for it. Ventura was warm and sunny year-round, and she loved it there and did not miss anybody at home very much, and never came back to visit. So when she died, alone, happy, in her home on Catalpa Avenue, the relatives raised the money to fly her body back and bury it in the cold ground of Looseleaf, North Dakota. All alone, by the back fence.
Mona Sparrow, 1915-1998.

12. A night on Lake Winnesissibigosh

And now they were at the airport, and the *Lucky Lady* was good and snowed-in. A stiff wind out of the northwest whipped the snow across the flats in eddies and a drift had formed around the plane's nose, almost up to the fuselage, and there were deep footprints through the snow to the stairs. He walked up and opened the door and heard loud static and blips from the radio and fragments of sentences, a distant male voice, very clipped and official. Buzz was sitting crosswise in the left-hand seat. Buddy was sleeping in the back of the plane. Buzz turned the volume down. James peered out the windshield. The lights at the end of the runway — gone. The revolving beacon atop the terminal — visible dimly.

"We're stuck, aren't we?"

Buzz nodded. "Turns out to be a bigger storm than what they thought," he said. "Two storms converged. Curvature of the jetstream flattened out and two fronts sort of intermixed. So we're not going to be moving anytime soon."

"Any estimate?"

"Your guess is as good as mine."

He walked back to the car slowly. It wasn't his way to make up stories but he needed an excuse not to go to Uncle Earl's bedside right now. The thought of it made him almost cry

— holding the old man's hand and — what? Saying the Lord's Prayer? Singing "Kumbaya"? He sounded chipper on the phone, but — what was the real deal? "I'm on this mission," he told Leo, "and it'd be better if it weren't general knowledge that I'm in town right now. It's very complicated. We're using the blizzard for cover. It's all a front. Confuse Can-Tell. Businessman snowbound. It's to throw them off. I wish I could tell you more. Is there an undisclosed location where I could spend the night and nobody be any the wiser?"

"I thought you were going over to Earl's."

"Tomorrow. Got to think of the mission first."

Leo thought for a minute. "Well, probably your best undisclosed location would be Floyd's fish house seeing as how he's dead. Faye still has them tow it out on the ice every year. Nobody ever uses it."

He could sleep the night in a dead man's fish house. Why not? Better than being a guest. He just plain wasn't up for a bunch of grief and hand-holding tonight.

"Where can I get some warm boots?"

"All of Floyd's stuff is out there. Help yourself. It's the fish house with the Christmas star on the roof. I'll drive you out there."

And Leo swung left at the next corner and a minute later he was driving onto the vastness of Lake Winnesissibigosh, heading for the fish houses out towards the middle of the lake, a long string of them, ghostly in the falling snow. The ice was 23 inches thick, according to Leo, yet it gave off banging sounds like an underwater howitzer, and Leo coasted to a stop. "I don't know about this," he said.

"It's nothing. Ice expands and contracts. Happens all the time. I grew up here. I remember."

"You sure?"

He was sure. He was pretty sure he was sure. On the other hand, he didn't have to stay out here. No. He had a cell phone, he could call the pilots and tell them he wished to spend the night aboard the *Lucky Lady* where the rear couch folded out to make a queen-size bed, but he couldn't do that with Leo there, listening. Let Leo think him a coward, a cake-eater. No way. He'd decided to be a C.I.A. agent — so he'd be a hero. No way out. He had to sleep in the fishing shack. Leo dropped him off a hundred yards from the shack — "Looks to me like there might be a soft spot up ahead" — and James climbed out. An electric star shone brightly on the fish house roof.

"Why'd he put that there?"

Leo said Floyd needed the star because he often was drunk.

"He lived out here?"

"If you were married to Faye, you might, too."

"Well —" said James, and Leo said, "Yeah. Guess I better head back." But he didn't move.

"Getting late," said James.

"Looks like it," said Leo.

"So anyway —"

"Good to have you back."

"Good to be back."

"Ten years is a long time to be away."

"Well, I don't really know anybody here —"

"Hard to know anybody if you never come around. I'm just saying."

"Yeah."

"Anyway —"

James thanked him and closed the car door and Leo did a big U-turn and headed for shore at a good clip and James stood in the enormous silence of the snowfall and looked across the snowy drifts on the broad reach of ice toward the lights of Looseleaf barely visible in the distance. He thought, "This is the beauty of an obsessive irrational fear like the one I got. You focus on that and your other fears recede. Probably men ran screaming into ferocious battle, into the teeth of the beast, swinging their broadaxes, who were terrified of spiders." General George S. Patton could not bear the sight of sheep. Lindbergh, flying the Atlantic solo in his little plane, was terrified of women. Genghis Khan rode horseback because he had a well-documented ant phobia. So he, James Sparrow, had benefited by this silly obsession that he had struggled manfully to overcome and consulted specialists about — psychiatrists, hypnotists, a nose-throat-and-tongue man at the Mayo, a yogi, hydraulic engineers, and so forth — but in fact his "pump problem" was a sort of magic that kept worse phobias at bay. He had never been a hypochondriac, never worried about business failure, never agonized over the lack of purpose in his life. *Be thankful for your afflictions.*

Some of them may be assets in disguise. Soon his nose was running and he felt an ache in his chest from the cold air. *Breathe through your nose, not your mouth,* said Mother. So lovely was the night, he kept right on walking out past Floyd's fish house toward the other shore. *Quite a day,* he thought. *You start out on the 55th floor of the Wabash Tower thinking you're going to take a trip to Hawaii and you wind up in an old wooden shack on a frozen lake in North Dakota.* The snow descended in a steady silent sound, a sort of continual hush. He walked almost to the bushy shore and then sensed something moving in the underbrush and a chill panic touched his heart. He turned around and walked, walked, walked — resisting the urge to run — to the shack with the Christmas star and opened the door and went in. A small dim room, plywood floor, two holes to fish through. A stove, a chair, a table, a broad shelf on one side to lie down on and beneath it, a cupboard. There was a hook on the door and he hooked it shut. He balled up some newspaper from a stack and stuffed it in the stove and lit it and got some kindling going and put in a couple birch logs and the place warmed right up. He got a little tin pot out of the cupboard and filled it with snow to melt to make tea in the morning. The fish house was quite cozy. He dug into the cupboard and found a half-full quart bottle of Paul Bunyan bourbon and a pint of peppermint schnapps, a few old *Playboys* ("lissome lonesome Kelly Jo, 23, lounges by the pool, sipping a cool limeade. 'Though it was my first time, I was quite relaxed about posing nude, having always felt that the body is a thing of beauty' "), a copy of a John Sandford novel, *Lamprey* ("the tall angry man hurtled past the line of patrons at the coffeeshop including a child of three or four years old like a cougar going for a snow rabbit and snarled, 'Gimme a java, toots,' at the startled barista, an attractive woman of perhaps twenty-four or twenty-five, and when an older woman behind him said, 'Uh, there is a line here, sir,' he turned and shrieked, 'You dumbheads can eat weasel poop for all I care,' and pulled out what appeared to be a .45 caliber pistol and fired two shots *bam bam* through the woman's left breast which flopped bleeding from her blouse like a small wounded animal such as a weasel or pocket gopher"), which he tossed in the fire, which flared up, and he dug out an old sleeping bag and laid it across the cupboard to sleep on and was about to crawl in when he heard snuffling outdoors and opened the door and walked out and looked around and turned to go back in the shack and there, sitting motionless beside the shack was a gray wolf in the light of the blue moon. His eyes were greenish-yellow and unblinking. His ears perked, his forelegs braced, his fur rippled. His tail lay curled and quite still. James stopped. A shock to see but deep in his brain his old Scout-master Elmer told him that, faced with a hostile dog (or, in this case, wolf) you must face him squarely and not attempt to run. No panic, no sudden moves. Square your shoulders and plant your feet and calmly look over the wolf's head as if observing something beyond. The animal had been waiting for James to come. That was his take on the situation. This was not happenstance. This was a personal encounter.

13. To his surprise, the wolf turns out to be someone he used to know quite well

If the wolf charged him, he decided not to assume the fetal position but let out a blood-curdling scream and crouch low and go for the beast's throat. He thought he felt a knife in the pocket of the parka, and he slipped his hand in and found it among the flotsam, the lengths of string, needlenose pliers, duct tape, and empty snoose can, a Bic pen, some lead sinkers, scraps of paper. He opened the knife. The blade was dull, but it would do. He withdrew it slowly and held it in his right hand hanging loosely at his side.

The wolf blinked. He had noticed. Good. A little zap of confusion in the animal's brain. It was fifteen feet to the wolf and fifteen feet to the door of Floyd's shack which, he reckoned, he could make in three seconds, but maybe that'd be too sudden. Better to take five seconds to stroll purposefully to the door and open it and slip inside. He guessed the shack was nothing the wolf cared to be part of. Probably it smelled horrible to him, the stench of man and his beverages and his dreadful urine.

"No, not horrible," said the wolf in a low whispery voice. "Once I was a man myself, like you. I remember the smells. Some of them with fondness. I remember your smell very well."

"Who are you, sir?"

"We used to camp out here overnight, you and me. There were eight or ten of us, all in one tent." The wolf glanced toward shore. "Over there by the marsh." The wolf spoke without moving his lips, the voice simply emerged from him.

"We were in Scouts together?"

"I am your age. Or I was when I died."

So it was Ralph.

They were standing on the spot where Ralph's canoe sank that chill October day in 1992.

He went out duck-hunting in his green wooden canoe, his big rubber hip boots on, and the canoe tipped and he plunged into the chill water and the hips boots filled up with water and he sank and drowned. They dragged the lake for him and two days later his body floated to the surface and drifted toward shore. Floyd found him. Floyd lifted this horrible mass of bloated flesh into his boat and laid his slicker over it and never went hunting again.

"How are you, Ralph?"

A silly question.

"I was a happy man with a sad life and you are a sad man with a happy life," he said. "Just for your information. You can put away the knife, James. You won't need it. I'm here to guide you, not attack you."

"I don't think I need a guide, Ralph. I'm doing okay on my own."

The wolf sneezed and then sneezed again. Or maybe it was laughter. He spoke slowly. "You are a frightened man and you live in vast ignorance. And now you've come to a place you never intended to be and there is more at stake here than you know."

James put the knife away. "Do you mind if we step inside?" he said. And the door to the shack swung open.

He put another birch log on the fire and got down a cup and poured whiskey in it.

"What happened to you that day, Ralph?"

"I was hunting, wading through the cattails, and I shot two ducks with two shots and they plunged into the water a hundred yards from shore. I could see them out there flapping and I got in my canoe to put them out of their misery. My old retriever Jackson had died in March and I grieved for him and it took me a while to get myself a pup and by the time hunting season rolled around, he wasn't trained in so I had to retrieve the birds myself."

"I remember, you always hunted alone."

"I did. I liked my friends well enough but I didn't go in for drinking in a duck blind and the bad jokes and the loud talk. They didn't care if they got game or not. I did. That was the point of it. I loved hunting. It wasn't about killing things, it was about the intense awareness when you sit perfectly still with eyes sharpened, nose to the wind, ears open, your whole being at attention. The hunter can sit for hours of keen attention, hearing every whisper and trickle, every bird chitter and fish splash, the drip of rain, the hush of twilight, the raccoons washing their paws, the little fox learning to make no sound, and why spoil it with the usual yikyak about the sorrow of growing old? Hunting is sacred: why else would you sit there in the cold and damp? It's all about that awakening of the visceral senses that get dull in the ordinary dry tedium of indoor paper-pushing and the meetings and the sucking up to big shots, and when you picked up a gun and went down to the tall grass, you got free of all that sucking and blowing. That's why I went, though I knew I should not, after Jackson died, killed by a car that didn't bother to stop. I loved that mutt. I thought I was over it but I wasn't. The moment those birds splashed down, my heart felt torn in two, and I paddled out from shore in blind grief, and I grabbed one duck and reached for the other and it squawked and flapped away, mortally wounded, and I wanted to end its pain and I swung at it with the paddle, broke its neck, and myself plunged overboard and I sank quickly, my heart full of regret for Theresa, and I managed to get one hip boot off but not the other, and I sank to the bottom into the mud down beside some turtles and when I awoke, it was dark and I was surrounded by furry things who were snuggling up next to me. I was in a beaver hut. An extended family of beavers, and they brought me bark and moss and lily pads and they put on ceremonies in which they crowned me with a headdress of small sticks and they sang and turned in circles and dipped and nodded in unison. They appeared to be worshipping me. I slept and slept and when I awoke, it was spring."

"What happened then?" said James.

"I worked in a Denny's in Fargo for

a few weeks, clearing tables, bussing dishes. And nobody spoke to me ever, though I kept asking them why I was there, and that's how I knew I was dead. Because I didn't exist. And I wasn't paid a penny. And one night a woman came and sat in a back booth and asked me to bring her a bowl of rice and beans. I told her I was only a busboy. She wore a blue suit with a gold badge that said *A.T.F.* and she was frightening to behold but beautiful. She said, 'Your old life is over and your new life is begun. You will spend a time grieving and treading the paths of your old life and seeing everything with clear eyes.' And she waved a hand in my direction and I became as you see me, a gray wolf. And so I have lived in the creek bed where we used to camp, observing my people, whom

I dearly loved, and who, though they are foolish, wasteful, of limited intelligence, and habitually cruel, I now love even more tenderly."

The wolf came over to James and lay his head on James's leg and said, "Every year during the Christmas moon, I have the power of speech and this is only the second time I've used it."

"What was the first?"

"I told Theresa that I loved her. She was horrified and slammed the door in my face."

The wolf's eyes filled with tears. "I didn't choose to leave the world and even now, years later, there are times I want to return. And Christmas is one of those times. Christmas and baseball season and the last week of August for the State Fair and the week in

April when the blossoms open up."

"I never cared for Christmas," said James.

"I know all about that. And it can't be changed."

"Why not?"

"You've made up your mind and it can't be unmade."

That came as a slap in the face to Mr. Sparrow who thought of himself as open-minded, reasonable, able to be moved and convinced by evidence, not some irredeemable dope, and he was about to protest — "It's only an *opinion* — maybe I need to take another look at the situation — read some books — maybe if I went to work in a soup kitchen for the homeless and got a different perspective" — but the sorrow in Ralph's eyes stopped him. And then he had a fearful thought.

"Ralph," he said. "Tell me. Have I died and landed in hell? Will I be here forever? Is this going to be perpetual winter? *Is this it, Ralph? Is this all there is?*" But the wolf was gone.

He opened the door and saw a flicker of tail in the underbrush. "Ralph!" he called. *"Ralph!"* Why had his old friend come to this harsh judgment?

And then girlish voices counting off *One-two-one-two-three* and there were Debbie and Becky and Ginny and Joni and Julie and Nanci and Lori and Gloria, the Looseleaf cheerleaders in their scarlet and gray middie uniforms and long socks and sneakers and pom-poms in hand and doing a vigorous version on ice of the old school song:

We're here to fight for Looseleaf
To the crimson team we're true.
You can cry and howl, and throw in the towel
Cause we'll tromp all over you (YOU BETCHA!)
We're going to win for Looseleaf
As you know darned well.
We are the Lucifers, the mighty mighty Lucifers,
And you can burn in hell. SSSSSSSSSSSS.

They were all 17 and 18 but their eyes were old, and when he spoke to them, they looked his way without recognition, and when he said their names, they hissed at him, *Sssssssssssss.* And then trotted off into the colony of fishing shacks and vanished.

A moment of blind panic. Maybe

this world was trying to tell him it no longer wanted him in it and that he should have flown to Hawaii because his decision to come here and bid a dying man good-bye was actually not so different from a dive off the Golden Gate bridge.

He could die here. That was a clear possibility. What to do?

What about a National Guard rescue by helicopter, or snowmobile? Maybe he could tell them about his pump-handle anxiety. Couldn't his analyst Dr. Boemer get word to the governor that Mr. James Sparrow, the head of Coyote Corp., was very likely to come unhinged if the Guard didn't go in and extract him from this storm?

He guessed not. The governor was a Democrat; Mr. Sparrow was not. And even if he could be persuaded to do it, the story would surely hit the papers:

MOGUL AIRLIFTED AT TAXPAYER EXPENSE WHILE DOZENS TRAPPED AWAIT RESCUE

"He suffers from a rare pump-handle obsession," says therapist, "and needs to go to a warm place."

NATIONAL GUARD CREW RISKS LIFE FOR TYCOON SO HE CAN SPEND HOLIDAYS AT HAWAIIAN ESTATE

Meanwhile, families in remote areas were at risk for hunger and snow-borne diseases.

14. In the terminal zone

He needed to settle himself down so he sang the old childhood song that Dr. Boemer had imprinted in him, using hypnosis, to relax him by unconscious reflex. It usually worked. He sang:

On the road to Mandalay
Where the flying fishes play
And the dawn comes up like thunder
out of China cross the bay.

But Mandalay was nowhere around

here. He returned to the fishing shack with a heavy heart and when he opened the door, he was in a vast room in an airport, a room as big as three 747 hangars and over the loud-speakers came a man's voice making important unintelligible announcements. James was standing in a long line of travelers waiting to speak to a woman with big black hair who sat on a high stool behind a counter under a sign, *External Travel.* She had several yellow pencils stuck in her hair and also a small telephone on a wire that went to a bud in her ear. She had very serious eyebrows.

The line was not moving. The man at the head of the line was speaking to her and sobbing and she looked at him impassively. He dabbed at his eyes with a hanky. He held out his arms, beseeching her, and she waved him away. The line inched forward. Next in line was a family, a woman and man and a little girl, and they seemed to have a long story to tell — it went on and on and on — and they were dismissed eventually — and then the woman behind them stepped forward and pulled out a violin and took her time tuning it and set up a music stand and a score and started to play. James said to the man in front of him, “Don’t these people realize there are others waiting in line behind them?”

The man turned around and said, “بلقلا .ادودحم نوكي ويذهب العمر ضعبل راظت ال ام”

“I’m sorry. Could you speak English?”

The man looked as if he’d been at the airport for days or weeks. Dark circles under his soft brown eyes. A dark stubble on his cheeks and jaw. A white shirt, open at the neck, rumpled. Black hair, gray at the temples.

"I hope we won't have to wait too long, that's all," said James.

The man touched his arm. "أن يمكن قودنص يف اهعضو يغبني ال هناو ةياهن كل شخص هو مقدس والتي ال." he said.

It took some time, during which James lay down on the hard floor and slept and dreamed about Boy Scouts and standing in a straight line with neckerchief tight, back straight, saluting, as the bugler played Taps, and then the man behind him kicked him and woke him up and he scootched forward and slept some more and was kicked and inched forward and kicked and inched, meanwhile dreaming about the tall grass, the precipice, the sharks in the black abyss below, the buzzards circling, and finally he was the second person in line — the man in front of him pleading to go to Chicago where his beloved daughter was waiting for him, she needed him, she loved him, he was her daddy, her precious daddy, but it was no soap, Big-Hair Lady sneered and shook her head, withdrew a pencil, scratched his name off the list. The man slumped down sobbing about the unfairness of it, and then it was James's turn.

"I too wish to go to Chicago. Or to Looseleaf, North Dakota. I seem to have jumped the tracks of my life and I'm in some strange void and I'd like to get back to my beloved wife and — I don't care about the money — or Hawaii — just want to see Joyce and get my life back. The familiar life. Okay?"

"Let me see your identification."

Well, of course he didn't have any. "I must've left it in my coat."

She was not interested in the idea of his not having identification. It didn't interest her in the slightest.

"Please," he said. "I'm a good guy. I'm a human being. Give me a break."

He might as well have said, "I am the ghost of William Tecumseh Sherman" or "I am a man who uses proper grammar" or "I represent the oppressed of the world." *Not of interest, sir.*

"My name is James Sparrow and I live in the Wabasha Towers with my wife, Joyce. I am the founder and CEO of Coyote Corp., makers of 4xPrime energy additive and the parent corporation of BRB and Sparrow Broadcasting and Sparrow Publishing. I am 42 years old and I am perfectly happy to give that all up, and the airplane too, if I can just get out of here so that I can celebrate Christmas."

She laughed a harsh metallic laugh like skillets clanging — "You? Celebrate Christmas? That'd be like a sheep dancing the schottische. Like a hawk writing a haiku. Be serious, sir."

"My wife is ill — I want to be with her for Christmas."

"Your wife is sick of you, is the problem."

"Please," he said. "It would mean so much —"

Big-Hair Lady threw back her head and screeched. "HA!!!" She shook her head. "Mister Sparrow, it would mean *nothing* to you. *Zero. Zilch. Nil. Ixnay.* You, sir, derive less real pleasure from this world than anybody who's ever come through here. You are blind and deaf and cold to the touch and you have no taste and music and poetry and good cooking are lost on you. You're all tied up in knots about money and getting old and the daily insult of the bathroom mirror. You walk down city streets with no eye for your fellow citizens, you are offered magnificent music and exit early so you won't get caught in traffic. You think happiness is somewhere out in the future but you have no more idea what it is than you could explain radioactivity. You are a man of stunning ineptitude. Your daddy knew about engines, plumbing, hydraulics and arc welding and pouring concrete, gutting a deer, cleaning a walleye, digging a fish hook out of your thumb, not to get rich but just to get by, and here you are and you feel superior to him and you can't pour piss out of a boot when the instructions are printed on the sole. You got your fortune because you walked into a bar in Livingston, Montana, just as a drunken chemist got really desperate, but that doesn't make you worth much in my book, mister. You walk through life like you're waiting for it to begin any day now. And it's almost over."

"Please, I'll do better." *Almost over??* What did she mean?

"Couldn't hardly do worse," she muttered, and scratched his name off the list. "I'm giving you twenty-four hours to go look around and make your peace. Go. Git. Scram. Out of my sight. And blow your nose, please."

He turned and ran out the door under the EXIT sign and there he was back on the ice outside Floyd's fishing shack. The stars shone in the sky, the other shacks were where they had been, the wind blew a little colder than before. He'd left his coat and mittens back there in the giant terminal and the wind was hard and sharp. He didn't dare go back for them lest the Big-Hair Lady revoke his pass. He stood on the ice, frozen between Forward and Reverse, and was starting to consider the option of freezing to death, when someone called his name. It was his cousin Liz.

15. James's inner resolve is sorely tested in the dark waters

"James, what the hell you doing out here?" He stepped toward her to give her a hug and warm up a little, and she didn't hug him back much, it was mostly all him. She was lean, wiry, a cross-country skier, who liked to ski in snowstorms and once, trapped in a storm, she dug a hole in a deep drift and stayed there for four days, wrapped in a thermal sheet like tin-foil, and was able, she claimed, to lower her heart rate and respiration to something like a state of hibernation and thus conserve her strength.

A true North Dakota woman.

"Leo said you were shitting bricks about getting snowbound and then you insisted on coming out and staying in Floyd's shack so I came to make sure you've got a decent sleeping bag." She walked over to the shack — he took a deep breath — and opened the door and did not disappear into the Other World — no Big Hair there, just the lantern and stove and the cupboard with the sleeping bag on it — and she shut the door.

"Looks like you're all set," she said. She looked him up and down. "Kind of cold to go out without a coat," she said. "Come on over to my shack, I'm just starting a fire." Her shack stood closer to shore, an 8x10 structure of weatherbeaten barn boards, smoke curling up from the stack. The woodpile next to it stood shoulder high. On the shack he could see several signs, EXTREMISM IN THE DEFENSE OF LIBERTY IS NO VICE and WHEN I HEAR THE WORDS *GUN CONTROL* I REACH FOR MY REVOLVER and NOW IS THE TIME FOR THE TREE OF LIBERTY TO BE WATERED WITH THE BLOOD OF TYRANTS.

Liz was a rabid Republican who believed that the U.S. government had secret agents on her trail, surveilling her with security cameras and satellites, ready to pounce at any time. She owned a steel helmet that deflected satellite rays and carried two loaded .45 pistols in her yellow down vest. Her house was kept hermetically sealed against bacteria that government agents might spray on the homes of patriots. She was a contributing editor of *Freedom* magazine and a leader of the citizen militia Possum Comatosis. She used 4xPrime and got along on two hours of sleep a night, a watchful sentry on freedom's ramparts. He liked Liz. He had always liked her since they were kids and played Three Musketeers in the court of Louis XIV of France and went swashbuckling around and being French, dueling with infidels — "Do me the honor, my good lord, of taking your sword from its scabbard," she cried and crossed swords with a phantom enemy and drove him down into the creek where he slashed her face, *Mon Dieu!* And she dropped her sword and sank to her knees in abject pain. And then snatched up the sword and drove it through the blackguard's heart. *Allons!* "Long live the king." And she was still caught up in swashbuckling except now against the government of the United States.

She opened the door to her shack and he walked in. It was dark except for the red glow from the firebox. At one end was a bench on an elevated platform. No fishing holes in the ice. And then he noticed, atop the firebox, a steel tray with rocks on it.

"I worry about you living down in Chicago and reading the mainstream press, James. You miss out on a lot." Liz believed that government is a relentless force seeking to imprison us in regulation and any person with a brain fights back, but Democrats, like the majority of people, are lazy thinkers and in the end some sort of armed uprising may be necessary to rescue the country from tyranny.

"Chicago's not bad. This town doesn't hold a lot of wonderful memories for me, Liz. This town gave me permanent nightmares and put me into therapy."

"What you in therapy for?"

He made the mistake of telling her. Pump handles.

"Oh you're not one of those, are you?"

He was, actually. He was winter-disabled. Some people had frost phobia or wind-chill anxiety and he had a pump-handle obsession. He tried to explain it to her, his powerful compulsion to put his tongue on an iron pump handle even knowing that the tongue would freeze to the iron instantly and he'd either have to wait for help to arrive — some Good Samaritan — "What's wrong, sir?" —

Mmmpfl rmnllglgl shrdllrgrgr — "I'm sorry, sir, I can't understand you" — so you count to three and pull away violently and rip the skin off. And that was why he lived in a high-rise apartment building and rode around in a chauffeured limo and avoided historic sites during winter months and salvage yards and playgrounds and when things got too bad, he flew to Hawaii.

"And I'm seeing a therapist," he said. "In fact, several of them."

"Listen, James. No jerk in an office with a bunch of certificates on the wall is going to talk you out of belief in your own demons. You got to face them yourself." Her daughter Angie was in treatment for recovery addiction, she said. Angie liked to drink so she went to AA because her boyfriend told her to and then she got to liking AA and went to different groups at different times of day and soon was up to 21 AA sessions a week, three a day, and was trying to cut down, and had joined an Addiction Recovery Dependency group.

Liz went outdoors and got an armload of wood and came back in and said she wasn't going to let him leave town until they had dealt with this pump-handle thing.

"I'm dealing with it."

"You're not dealing with it. I'm family, James. I can tell you things other people can't. You're full of b.s. and you need to clean out your system and that's what we're going to do now."

"I don't know what you're talking about."

She grabbed a shovel from the wall

and went outside and he followed — she walked over to a big rectangle cut in the ice and started punching at the thin ice that had frozen over it. And turned to him and told him to take his clothes off and follow her into the sauna.

"Aha," he said. And then she grabbed the zipper on her big insulated jumpsuit and pulled it from her neck down to her left ankle and stepped out onto the ice naked. His cousin Liz. Her left breast was missing. Just scar tissue. "I had it cut off," she said. "It got in my way when I aimed a rifle."

She opened the shack door and now billows of steam came blowing out and in she went. He stepped out of his boots and took off his shirt and pants and stood barefoot on the ice, a strong sensation, pain and then numbness, and a moment of decision, *Yes — No — Stay — Go —* and his life seemed to hang in the balance — a wrong move could lead to oblivion — *Why am I standing here? I am worth millions of dollars. I don't need this at all.* — A man in his jockey shorts in a stiff wind. *What is this leading to? Run! Beat it! Scram! Get out of here! This woman could eat you for breakfast.* And then he stripped his shorts off and walked to the door. *I am a prisoner here and I am not going to give her the satisfaction of seeing me beg for mercy. For the honor of Chicago and of liberals everywhere* — he opened the door and stepped into a cloud of steam in pitch blackness and closed the door. It was hot in there. Hotter than hot. It scorched his face. *Damn it is hot.* He took a shallow breath. He could see her pale form sitting on the bench and on the firebox, the rocks glowed red-hot coals. A pail alongside. "Throw some water on," she said. He picked up the pail and sloshed water on the rocks — "Not so much" — he was about to say *Sorry* and caught himself. "In Chicago," he said, "we like a wet sauna. But whatever you like, Liz."

"Oh," she said. "Dry saunas, a person can tolerate longer, that's all."

And in that moment he knew he could best her. The tone in her voice. She'd expected him to come whimpering and cringeing into her torture chamber and he'd come marching in as a veteran, welcoming punishment.

"Wet saunas are more intense, but when in Rome —"

He plopped down beside her.

"Want a towel?" she said.

"Don't need one." He could hardly breathe. He didn't know how long he could sit here before his body burst into flame but he was going to sit still right up to the moment of combustion. "This is great," he said. Sweat poured from him, salt stung his eyes. He wanted to weep for pain.

"Glad you like it." There was defeat in her voice. It thrilled him. Her hair hung limp on her bare shoulders, she was hunched forward — and then he saw the birch boughs on the bench beside him.

"Ready for some stimulation?"

She started to turn around and he grabbed the boughs and lashed her four, five, ten times, fairly hard. "Hard enough?" he said. "Or do you like it more brisk?"

"That's fine," she said. So he lashed her harder. It felt good. He hit her in behalf of Hubert Humphrey, Jimmy Carter, Walter Mondale, and Michael Dukakis, and she trembled — "Too hard?" he cried. "No," she whimpered. He lashed her good until she cried out, "Thank you. How about you?" and then he jumped up and said, "Time for a swim!" and out the door he went. Steam poured off him in the cold air and pure red-blooded Triumph was in his heart and what is physical pain compared to Triumph? The freezing air blazed on his skin. He strode toward the big dark hole, Liz following a few steps behind him — his body was screaming at him *Don't do this! We don't like this! Bad idea! Bad idea!* — but in his heart he knew he was right: *Show No Weak-*

ness! No Indecision! He turned toward Liz and she put an arm over her one breast and a hand over her crotch — "This is great!" he cried. "How did you know I love saunas?" — and turned toward the hole with the same holy devotion as the Christian martyrs stepped into the arena — *All or Nothing!* — and took three quick steps and launched out — *Lord Jesus Christ into Thy Hands I commend my spirit* — into the cold blackness and it shocked him like a sledgehammer — but not in a bad way! No no no — his skin was freezing and his teeth chattered but the core of him was hot and between the two sensations was a center of equilibrium of pure feeling and high happiness and he yelled, "It's great! It's beautiful!" which made her hesitate. She stood naked in the twilight, vulnerable and defeated, and he cried, "Thank you, Jesus! Washed in the blood of the Lamb! Hallelujah!" She thought he was crazy. *Good.* He whooped and yelled some more. She was steeling herself to jump but she had lost her momentum and then he put his hands on the ice and hoisted himself up and stood and hugged her and she almost collapsed from the shock. Her thin, trembling body in his grasp. "Praise God from Whom all blessings flow," he said and he threw her into the water. She let out a pitiful *Eeeek* and he turned away and went into the shack. He put a fresh log in the fire and tossed water on the stones. She was right. He needed a breakthrough and he had broken through. He was all over the pump-handle business. Cured. He had stepped through that door and into the next room, which was beautiful and luminous and shimmering with delicate delights and in that moment he longed for his dear darling wife and wished she were in his arms, her strong shoulders, her broad naked back, her long legs, her sweet face turned up toward his, her Roman nose and dark hair pulled back, her smile, he wanted to kiss her smile and inhale her sweet voice.

16. Awakening to a new morning, he starts to feel at peace with the world

He lay down to sleep in Floyd's shack but was kept awake by feelings of transcendence and finally arose and put a couple logs on the fire, and made tea. He did his stretching exercises. He wanted to call Mrs. Sparrow and tell her he was cured of anxiety now but it was only 6:00 A.M. Five voicemail messages. The first was Simon expressing concern about the storm, and a second one inquiring about Mr. Sparrow's whereabouts, a third expressing some urgency about his whereabouts, and a fourth from a Captain McIver of the state police asking him to phone immediately. And the fifth was from her. Her calm and delicate voice. "I just called to say that I am missing you tons and tons and still feeling sort of under the weather so probably Kuhikuhikapapa'u'maumau is out of the question for me, darling, and it hurts me to say this, but I know how much you want to be there and so even though I miss you like crazy, I hope you'll go and have a beautiful Christmas, darling. You deserve it. A beautiful and peaceful Christmas, and I love you. I love you so much."

He was hungry and he headed for town across the ice, walking briskly through the falling snow, a new man now, and he wondered if the Big-Hair Woman was going to come after him tonight or if the jump in the lake had maybe won his release from her powers. He wasn't sure. He walked up on shore and down the street where the Thackers lived and the Enghs, but there were new names on the mailboxes now, Gant and LaFever. Nobody he knew. The name of Sparrow had vanished, too. Brother Benny hanging on in Alaska, running a camera shop financed by James, and Elaine, sad, worn down, alcoholic, in Fort Wayne, living on the checks he sent her every month, two victims of loser romances, bad habits, and no luck whatsoever, and meanwhile everything your big brother touches turns to gold. Unfair. You're drowning and people pass overhead drinking champagne on a hot-air balloon.

He walked in the Bon Ton Café,

stomped the snow off his shoes and parked himself at the counter, feeling mightily empowered. Far to the west, his Hawaiian house awaited him, the floodlights on the roof illuminating the plane of grass and the beach beyond and the white surf, but he was not done with North Dakota yet. An old man stood peering out the big window. "This isn't over yet," he said. "We're gonna see a lot more of this before it's over. Where you come in from?"

"Chicago."

"You gotta be lost."

James shrugged.

"Not as bad as the storm of '75. That was a bad one. January. Roads were closed for eleven days. Eleven. Thirty-foot drifts. Empire Builder train got stuck thirty miles west of

Minot and it took a week to dig those people out. There were children conceived on that train, that's how bad it was. Eighty m.p.h. winds, thirty-five died in North Dakota alone, and you know something? Most of them were glad to go. That's how it was." He took a sip of coffee. "Coffee's cold, Myrt." The waitress took a carafe off the hot plate and brought it over.

"Right here in town, a man and a woman were struggling through the storm to get home and finally they made it into the house and she looked at him and she'd never seen him before in her life. She said, 'You're not Bob.' He said no, he was Larry. She said, 'Where'd my husband go?' He said he didn't know, that he saw her reach out her hand so he took it. She said, 'I wonder what happened to Bob.' He said he had no idea. She said, 'Well, as long as you're here, you may as well come in and get warm.' And he did. And they're still together. Had three children. Bob never came home. That was in 1975. January. Sure tells you something about marriage, doesn't it."

The wind whistled in the weather-stripping, just like it did in their house when he was a kid. Cold drafts. Once, Daddy woke up in the night, deaf in his left ear — it had been frozen by a cold draft. Never got better.

A man in a snowmobile suit sat on a stool at the counter and Myrt slid a cup in front of him and filled it with java from the carafe in her right hand.

"You don't take cream, do you, Bobby?"

"You know me better than

that, Myrt."

"Oh yeah. It's your brother who takes cream. How's he doing in Florida?"

"He's stuck there, that's what. Paid three-quarters of a million for a house that's now worth about half that and he lost his job and he's working part-time as a security guard."

"You ever been to Florida?"

"Why would I want to go there?"

"It's warm there."

"If you're cold, put on a sweater. That's what I say."

"I've got two on already."

The snowmobile suit and the waitress didn't look at James but they were thinking about him, he could tell. They were aiming their repartee in his direction.

"Another reason not to go to Florida, Myrt: no ice fishing."

"I could live without it if I tried. Nothing but an excuse to drink, if you ask me."

"Man has to keep off the chill any way he can."

"My brother never drank at home. A cocktail was foreign to Marvin, strange as an artichoke, but he'd go ice fishing and when they passed the Four Roses he took a hit off it. And that was when he ran off with that woman. She was lost, or so she said, and came out to the fish house to get warm, and he warmed her up all right. Took her off to a motel and turned the heat up. And it all started with taking a drink."

"I never knew your brother but I do know that a lot of people have perished in winter storms for want of a little whiskey. The death toll among Baptists is staggering."

"The woman he ran off with was a Baptist. Or married to a Baptist."

"Well, there's your motivation right there."

"I forget — did you say you wanted cream in your coffee?"

"Get away from me with that cream pitcher, Myrt."

The old man who was an authority on winter had moved over to the counter to get away from drafts. He motioned to Myrt for another cup of coffee. "Gimme the usual." He looked over toward James. "Man's got to keep up his strength in cold weather. Back in 1957, the temperature dropped forty degrees in one minute. Went from thirty-two to eight below. Sixteen teenagers were taken to the hospital. No scarf, no mittens, no warm jacket. Same winter we got ten feet of snow and a dozen houses collapsed from the weight on the roofs."

The phone rang. It was Buzz, at the airport. They had slept aboard the *Lucky Lady* and were eating cold pizza for breakfast. "Visibility is a hundred feet. The runway is iced over. Same with the fuselage and wings. The forecast is for nothing good whatsoever. The Interstate is strewn with abandoned vehicles. They're opening schools for shelters. Nothing to do but sit tight. You at your uncle's?"

"Staying at an undisclosed location, Buzz. Trying to get the situation under control, and map out the perimeter."

"Yes, sir."

Sitting tight sounded good to him.

He'd spent a good night out on the lake and nobody knew where he was and that was a first for him. A solo flight.

"I looked into the possibility of renting snowmobiles but nobody here thinks it's a good idea. Not with visibility like this," Buzz said.

"We'll just sit tight and see what happens," he said.

"Sorry about this, sir. Storm came up faster and harder than what they predicted. I should've been a little more cautious, in retrospect."

"Not a problem."

"I know how anxious you were to get to Kuhikuhikapapa'u'maumau."

"Kuhikuhikapapa'u'maumau will still be there next week."

At the mention of Kuhikuhikapapa'u'maumau, Myrt, Bobby, and

the old man looked straight at him and you could see the question forming in balloons over their head but they didn't ask. That was Looseleaf, for you. Stoicism, through and through, to the point of stupidity. No surprise, no alarm. Act like it's nothing. Blizzard, robbery, major coronary — *hey, no problem. Everything's under control.*

And then his phone rang again. A local number. He had a hunch who it might be — the Ojibway storyteller arisen before dawn to await the sun, and he didn't want to talk to her, not at all — but he had been given twenty-four hours to make his peace and he intended to do that. He opened the phone. "Hi, Faye," he said. "How's tricks?"

"Jimmy," she said. "I've been up

for hours, saying empowering prayers for you and lighting Shoshone vision sticks. Liz called me at 4:00 A.M. and said you are suicidal. She said you stripped off your clothes and jumped into the lake and she had to dive in and pull you out. What is going on? I love you. We all love you and we support your journey, wherever it may lead, but don't choose the Death Mother, Jimmy. Don't embrace the Great Bear of Perpetual Solitude. If there's anything we can do to help you return to your deeper self you only need ask. I am so very very happy you felt free to use Floyd's fishing shack, Jimmy. It was his spirit house, I know it welcomed you. Thank you, thank you, thank you. *Namaste.* The divine in me salutes the divine in you and thanks you for integrating your consciousness with his. He is still there, don't you think? Didn't you feel it? I do. Did you see the wolf? He was Floyd's best friend. I keep wishing the wolf would communicate with me. And sometimes I've gone out there at night and heard a woman trying to tell me something."

"A big-hair woman?"

"I don't know but she's telling me to make my peace with the world and that's what I'm trying to do. Come over, Jimmy. I need to see you." So he zipped up his parka and, though he hadn't ordered any breakfast, he slipped a $20 bill under a used coffee cup on the counter. Myrt was watching his reflection in the toaster. She didn't miss a trick. He headed for the door and she was on the twenty like a bald eagle on a bunny.

17. A séance with Faye

Faye was a fool but sometimes fools have a good message for us in among their foolishness and so James steeled himself with a cup of coffee and marched down to Faye's little house with the wind chimes dinging and tinkling on the front porch and the sign on the front door, *Abandon Fear and Prejudice, All Ye Who Enter Here,* and knocked on the door. She was right there, waiting for him. "Come in," she cried. "Oh you look exhausted. Oh it is good to see you!" She took some white powder from her pocket and tossed it over his left shoulder and the right and dropped some at his feet and then hugged him. "You and I are kinsmen, Jimmy. We are family. We are interconnected whether we know it or not. We nurture each other with our common myths and rituals and in each other we find a wholeness of wisdom."

He heard water dripping from a waterfall trickling into a plastic pond with several rather lethargic goldfish. A teakettle whistled in the kitchen and she went to make them a pot of tea. Her hair had an ethereal, see-through red color. He noticed when she turned her back that she'd put on weight. She wore a big white frilly dress and it was broad in the beam. Interconnected or not, the woman was eating like a horse. On the walls were large color photographs — three feet by four — landscapes — corn stubble, a snowy field, a creekbed with three big cottonwood trees rising from it, an abandoned farm site, another abandoned farm site, and then a full frontal view of a naked woman of advanced years, in black-and-white. He didn't want to look at it but it was hard not to. "That's a self-portrait," she said. He had guessed as much. "It took me forty years to get up the courage to do that," she said. He thought it might've been better if she hadn't waited so long but he didn't say anything.

"I have so much I want to share with you," she said. A crystal chandelier hung from the ceiling. A low ceiling and an enormous chandelier, so you had to walk around it. She had glued various clay figures to the chandelier, horses and bears, some Indian figures, a couple of coyote. "I bought that in Tucson," she said. "And then when Floyd died, I moved back here because his spirit is here and my work is here." She was storytelling in schools and doing some life-coaching and trying to earn extra money by selling Greenspring organic skin cleanser, moisturizer, eye liner, mascara, and blush, and her sister Liz was boycotting her because some of the products were made in Communist China, so she and Liz were not speaking, but they had often not spoken in the past so it was no hardship.

"How's your Christmas?" he said.

"Oh Jimmy," she said. "Don't you feel it? Christmas is the force field of heightened possibility. It's not about religion, those myths we were brought up with are only tools to direct us toward the mystery of the under self. It's about the ecstatic visualization of psychic metaphor. The psychic world is calling us toward balanced consciousness. Don't you feel that? There is a lightness and spontaneity that is struggling to get through all the commercial static and lead us out of our linear consciousness into a global wholeness. You know about global wholeness, don't you?"

He nodded. Yes, of course. "I feel so connected to you right now," she said. He sensed a hug coming on and he edged away.

She collected spoons and cups. Spoons, she explained, represented the generosity of life. So did cups. Hundreds of them hung on hooks on the wall. Wooden spoons, steel spoons, shallow spoons, deep spoons. "I want this to be good for you spiritually, coming back to Looseleaf, I know you came to see Daddy but really I think you've come here to find yourself, and I want to help you if I can. I've become a bard, Jimmy. A visionary conversationalist.

"My roots are here. Like yours, Jimmy. And I went away, as you did, because I felt a polarization between myself and my family. I had to live away until I was ready to come back. And when I was, then I was ready to find the road to spiritual growth in the beautiful motherness of the North Dakota prairie. My consciousness simply had to evolve from a reliance on mountain wisdom to a trust in prairie wisdom. There are visionary mother spirits here who want to guide us, but we need to be open to dialogue and the goal of transforming consciousness and opening the winter veil to evolutionary experience that nurtures the diversity of the heart that can make us whole."

She wanted to tell him the story of how she got started telling Ojibway tales and he got up from the table. "Back in a minute," he said, and headed for the door.

"It's cold out there!"

"I know. Gotta start the car."

"Scooter's going to come and start it."

He pretended not to hear her. He got into the parka and barreled out the door. It was brutally cold. He checked WeatherX on his phone and it said *Minus 38.* His big boots crunched in the snow like walking on cornflakes.

The painful sound of cars being started who only wanted to die. But she was right. He had come here to find himself. The bears were in their dens, the honeybees in their hives, the rabbits were browsing in the snow along with the squirrels, their hieroglyphic tracks were everywhere, and he belonged here as much as any of them.

Forty-two years ago, in Fargo, his mother was nine months, two weeks, and ten minutes pregnant and his jittery father thought she should head for the hospital just in case, since the radio was talking about a blizzard, but she said no, she wanted to watch "The Dupont Christmas Cavalcade with Milton Berle, Fred Waring and His Pennsylvanians, and Kukla, Fran and Ollie" on their old Muntz TV and besides, the hospital was only thirteen blocks away, so she got herself comfy on the couch with a big bowl of buttered popcorn and a gallon of Dad's root beer. When the blizzard rolled in, Daddy got in a royal panic, charging to and fro and hollering about how nobody ever listened to him around here, and that brought on the labor pains. He walked her to the car and a wave of pain hit her and she screamed, which unnerved Daddy so that he drove the wrong way through the blizzard, and thirty-seven miles later, realizing his error, he made a U-turn right into the ditch. He ripped off his car door and lay Mother on it and slid her through the storm to a farmhouse where James Monroe Sparrow arrived, delivered by an old farmwoman with a basin of hot water and some clean rags, shouting at Mother in Polish to squat over the clean towel and *push,* meanwhile the farmwoman went out and strangled a chicken with her two knobby hands and made chicken soup. Mother groaned and tiny James wailed, the midwife cut the umbilicus with a paring knife and taped it with duct tape, and then she looked around for Daddy, he had gone to the cellar to get away from the yelling and gotten into the slivovitz and now, three sheets to the wind, he was on his way to shovel out the car, wearing only a white shirt and trousers. She clubbed him with a rolling pin and barricaded him in a closet and likely saved his life. The story was in the news and they were too embarrassed to go back to Fargo so they went to Mother's hometown of Looseleaf and Daddy got a job with Uncle Earl at the power plant. He was the bookkeeper.

Winter made James feel like a child. *Trapped.* In Looseleaf, winter came hard and fast; in a few days the world turned brown and gray and the house creaked as it shrank. Snow fell, then more and more. And more. The lake froze over and it sounded like gunfire, the ice hardening. Blizzards blew down from Canada and came in suddenly and unexpectedly. There was no weather forecasting, just a strong sense of foreboding — old Great-Aunt Cooter sitting by the wood stove, an old snaggle-toothed crone wrapped in tattered quilts, grizzled, rheumy-eyed, gumming her food, tobacco juice dripping down her chin, listening to the wind in the chimney, and she'd hoist herself up and roll her blue-gray eyes and croak like a tree toad, *It's a gonna be a bad one, chillun*. That was the forecast. And it always was a bad one. The town lay on flat open prairie, no windbreaks, just barbed wire, and the sky turned a metallic gray and got very low overhead and two or three feet of snow fell for a day or two and the wind blew it horizontally so that you could not see your hand in front of your face. And then the temperature dropped. To the manly men of North Dakota, winter was a challenge. Zero was considered a mild chill. Twenty below was cold. Forty below was darned cold. At sixty below you had to take precautions. They bundled up and went out to start the car which was frozen solid in the driveway. They put on a great mackinaw and four-buckle overshoes and cap with earflaps and out into the storm they went and when they raised the hood it screeched so loud the icicles fell off the house, huge forty-five-pounders like giant daggers of ice crashing and splintering.

James hid in a little nest in a crawl space up over the kitchen. It was warm in there and he ran an extension cord to plug a lamp in and he lay on old car cushions under Army blankets and read books from the library, pounds of them, books about Africa and India and the Amazon, and sailing on a tramp steamer to New Guinea and Czarist Russia and the Count and Countess Ouspenskaya in their palace and the lovely Ludmilla with her high cheekbones and Prince Sergei with the flashing blue eyes awaiting the revolutionaries who will attack in the morning and interrupt their beautiful romance, but tonight Ludmilla in her diaphanous white gown is playing Chopin in the drawing room for the young man in the cavalry uniform whose blue cigar smoke drifts through the candlelight and he steps out onto the terrace and snow is falling all across Russia, snow is general, and the delicious summer and fall have ended and now the grim winter of terror and desolation has begun, and outside he could hear Daddy calling his name, angry, demanding that he come downstairs immediately and start shoveling and help start the car.

And now here he was, thirty years later and two blocks away, feeling pretty good despite wind chill of minus eighty. He got in Faye's old Buick and it started right up and her radio came on. Public radio. A psychologist talking about feelings of alienation experienced during cold snaps and how people can combat this by dressing warmly. While the engine ran, James swept the walk, and then stood, the sting of cold air in his nose, and felt exhilarated. Especially when he spotted the old pumps in the yard next door. The man collected antiques and he had six pumps, their handles at five o'clock, waiting for someone doomed by fate to put a tongue on them but James was no longer that man. He was free. He went back into the house.

"I met the wolf and he's Ralph, my old friend who drowned duck-hunting when he was twenty-five. I am hoping to see him again. And I am on a twenty-four-hour pass from the spirit world to make my peace with everyone, and I have no idea what happens after that."

Faye hugged him. She held him close. Nothing she said had ever made much sense to him and yet there was some sort of fundamental goodness in her that appealed to him, much as he had always made fun of it in the past. She was a good woman in her own fogbound way. "I love you, Faye," he said. She thought about that for a long moment, perhaps waiting for him to say more, maybe something about global wholeness. Then she said, "I love you, James."

18. He meets his dying uncle who is in fine fettle indeed

He left Faye's and passed Uncle Boo's house and remembered the smell of peppermint schnapps and across the street was Uncle Sherm's who sat on that porch night after night, stone-faced, smelling of mothballs, his hair matted, and all he said was "Is that so?" and "How 'bout that?"

Second Coming was this morning, Uncle Sherm. *Is that so?* Jesus came and took all the believers to heaven for an eternity of bliss. *How 'bout that?* Everyone in the family except you and me, Uncle Sherm. *Is that so?*

But meanwhile we can drive their cars and eat all their frozen steaks. *How 'bout that?*

Through the falling snow, he saw Uncle Earl's little red-roofed bungalow nestled in big drifts with narrow canyons where the walks had been shovelled. Heavy plastic was nailed over the storm windows for extra insulation. A few lights were on inside and on the front porch was a jumble of electrical cables and fuse boxes and generators. Earl liked to keep his hand in. James opened the front door and a wave of warmth rolled out and the smell of baked chicken. But not ordinary chicken. This had special spices in it. The living room seemed more orderly than he remembered. The antimacassar on top of the old upright piano was spotless and the busts of Schumann, Chopin, Bach, and Mozart had been shined up. The red throw on the old green sofa was straight, the copies of *North Dakota Geographic* were neatly stacked, the fish tank bubbled away, the goldfish maneuvered through the plastic vegetation, and the carpet where Uncle Earl liked to strew his books was clear — the books were lined up on the bookcase, a sure sign that the occupant of the house was no longer in charge. Aunt Myrna's collection of china birds had been dusted. From the kitchen came a wave of wonderful chicken aroma — someone, he guessed it might be Oscar's wife, had opened the oven door and squirted butter on it. He called out, "Hello?" and a dark woman's face peered around the corner. She was short and fat and wrapped in red silk and wore large thin loops of gold around her neck. Her black hair was tied into two braids with a silver thread braided into it. Silvery shapes of sheep and goats were woven into the red silk wrap. She wore gilded sandals.

"I'm James Sparrow, I'm Uncle Earl's nephew from Chicago."

She bowed. "My name is Rosana," she said. "I am his caregiver. He is all excited about you coming. He's in the toilet now."

The kitchen had been scrubbed and polished way beyond the norm. The wood floor shone and two red rugs had been laid down by the breakfast nook. For years, the nook had been a holding area for stuff in transition, but now it was back in business again. Two thin blue tapers in silver holders, two red woven placemats — it was as if he had found a new wife.

Rosana was of indeterminate age. Indian, apparently. She was doing a fine job of making a martini, chipping the ice cubes, chilling the glass in the freezer, as she said, "Oh my, yes. I have heard very much good about you. All of it good. A very very rich man, are you not. Oh yes. He talks of you many many times. Many times. How you fly around to all the places in your aeroplane and go to a place and stay there and then to another and another. Goodness, yes. Much traveling you do. Yes, of course, because you must oversee your many business enterprises. That is very good. Very important. Oh my yes. How very very lucky for us that you include us in your busy travels,

Mr. Sparrow.

"But I talk too much. Here I am zipping my mouth with the zipper of silence and I am locking it shut and now I am putting the key in my pocket until you tell me to talk."

"Okay. Thank you."

"Please converse with your dear uncle, Mr. Sparrow, knowing that you shall have the silence you require. I am being still now."

"Thank you."

"Rosana will be quiet until you tell me to talk. Then I will talk. But now I am quiet. I will observe your wishes in the matter. And would you also wish a martini?"

It was ten A.M. Early for a martini. But why not? "Of course."

So she chilled a second glass and chipped more ice, and then there was a rustle and a low chuckle and Uncle Earl appeared, in blue bathrobe, pajamas, and slippers, thinner and paler but moving forward on his own power. A bad case of bed hair but the moustache was trim and the pajamas were clean. James stepped up and put his arms around him. He had shrunk somehow; the towering figure of James's youth had become dwarflike, but he still twinkled like the good old uncle of old. And he was carrying a plastic bag with a tube that seemed to be stuck in his abdomen.

"So you met my new girlfriend then?"

"You're a lucky man, Uncle Earl. She's taking good care of you."

"Eighty-six and I'm still attractive to the ladies, James."

Rosana poured the gin into the

shaker and a dash of vermouth and put the cap on and shook it, and Uncle Earl twitched his hips in a sort of mambo. The plastic bag in his hand made a squoshy sound.

"I heard you were at death's door, Uncle Earl."

"They were all set to put me in the ground, James. They bought the charcoal briquets to make the fire to heat up the ground so they could dig the grave. The coffin was on order from Grand Forks. The doctor had his death certificate all filled out except for the date and time. And then the county welfare office told us we were eligible for home hospice care and Liz was telling them no and I raised my head up off the pillow and said I wanted to die at home, and so they sent Rosana. A miracle worker. She got here and drove the death squad out and made me a martini and I've been in tall clover ever since."

"It is as God wills it to be," she said, ducking her head modestly, smiling, and she poured the liquor into the two glasses and put them on a tray with a dish of chips and a greenish dip and led the way into the living room.

"I've got a plane at the airport, Uncle Earl. Soon as this storm blows over, we could fly you out to Hawaii. I've got a place out there."

"I saw Hawaii when I was in the service. Honolulu. Gyp joints and dance halls and girls hanging on you begging you to dance with them and buy them a $50 bottle of $5 champagne. No need to go back and see it again."

"Or we could fly you to the Mayo

Clinic and see if they can't address some of your health issues."

"I'm eighty-six years old. I used up my time. But I made up my mind I want to go out with a big party. And here you are. So we're going to put away the black crepe and have us a big Christmas. And maybe a New Year's. And then I'm ready to go."

The old man followed Rosana into the living room and sat down in his big green armchair and she spread a comforter on his lap and turned an electric heater on his feet and lit a couple of candles and handed him his martini.

"What's in the plastic bag, Uncle Earl?"

"What? This?" The old man looked down at the bag in his hand as if he'd forgotten all about it. "It's my liver and pancreas, James. They were going to do a transplant, but they discovered, after they got it out, that the other liver wasn't the right shape, so they're waiting for another donor, and meanwhile, got my liver here in the bag, along with the pancreas, and they're working okay. Not great, but okay."

James was going to say something about Mayo doing great work in transplants, but decided not to. He looked out the window at the Christmas lights on the rambler across the street, a thousand of them burning bright through the night.

"That's the Guntzels. When he turns them all on at night, I get phone conversations on my radio. I was listening to one when you came in. Man telling his mother why his family couldn't come for Christmas this year and it was all a tissue of lies about these other things they had to do. Ha. They couldn't come because they didn't want to come, was the truth of the matter, and the old lady kept trying to fix it so they could. It was sad."

James sat down and smelled the gin. "I just saw Faye. She looks pretty good."

"That's her art on the wall." James looked over at a canvas with white drips spackled onto it, entitled *Beginnings, Endings, Connections, Continuations.*

"She doesn't earn much money from her art but she enjoys it."

"And Oscar?"

"We don't see much of him in the winter months. He just sort of slows down and he wasn't going fast to begin with."

"And Liz?"

"Busy saving the country from totalitarianism, last I heard. Where you staying by the way? I'd have you stay here, James, but Rosana's got the guest room."

"It's okay. I've got a place to stay."

They sat in silence for a while and the old man's eyes closed. James thought, *What if he croaks right now?* The old man's chest seemed to be moving but he couldn't tell. *At what point should I go over and listen for a heartbeat?* And then Uncle Earl smiled and said:

"I had a Swedish grandpa who went crazy here one winter. It was before there were snowplows and he stayed out on his farm for five months straight because he believed there was gold on his land and he didn't want anybody to steal it. There wasn't any, and we never could figure out how he came to think there was some, but he was convinced he was sitting on fields of gold. Maybe he read it in a book. His kids he had boarded with families in town so they could attend school and his wife stayed there to see to them, and he was snowbound on the farm week after week through one blizzard after another, living in the kitchen and burning as little wood as he needed to stay alive, feeding the livestock, nobody to talk to, and when they found him in the spring, he was extremely uncommunicative and there was madness in his pale blue eyes. He got himself cleaned up and went to church and plowed his fields but he was mad, and when summer rolled around he got to drinking fermented blackstrap molasses and stayed out late howling at the moon and came home with blood and feathers around his mouth. They sent him to the state hospital in Jamestown and put him in leg irons and my mother wouldn't let us go visit him but I snuck away, I felt it was my duty, and I found him in a little room, chained to his bed, and he was happy in his own mind, he was living in a castle in Fargo with forty-three servants to wait on him and he was going to spend the winter in Hawaii. He had a pineapple ranch there. It was all clear in his own mind. The state hospital didn't exist for him. That room with the peeling plaster walls was all a fiction. He was going to Hawaii."

It was a good martini.

"There was a lot of insanity going around. I remember the faith healer who came to warm us up one winter. From Texas. Waco, Texas. Presbyterian. All a matter of faith, he said. He was a thin man with deep-set eyes, wore a seersucker suit and a straw hat, carried his stuff in a cardboard suitcase, walked into various people's homes and cried out in tongues and tied fishline to their wrists and sprinkled sparkle dust around them and around Halloween it got down into the fifties, too cold for him, and he was shivering so bad, he couldn't wash nor shave nor button a button, and he lay there under a mountain of quilts and pleaded with us to give him money for a train ticket home, and we held out until the middle of November and we got tired of having to bring him his meals in bed and we sprang for a one-way ticket to Dallas. We had to drive him to Bismarck to catch the train and we had to put a fat girl on either side of him to keep him warm. And he lost his faith then and there. North Dakota winter made him question the existence of a loving God. He went back to Texas and learned to shuffle a deck of cards so as to put the cards he needed in a place where he could find them. He earned his living playing Texas-draw poker in the back rooms of pool halls and he had beautiful women to keep him warm and the last we heard, he'd been elected to Congress."

Uncle Earl sat and beamed at him and sipped his gin. "It's good to have you here."

"Sorry I haven't been back to visit

you. I meant to." James stared at the plastic bag, wondering what a liver and pancreas looked like. Did he dare ask for a peek?

Uncle Earl waved away the apology, like a mosquito. "It's okay." He beamed some more. For a man who was about to dive underground, he was in a highly jovial mood. "You were a good kid, James. Your mother and dad worried so much about you they never got to enjoy you, but I did. And now look at you. You're the biggest thing to ever come out of this town."

"The bigger they are, the harder they fall."

Uncle Earl thought about this for a moment. "I could've done more with my life but I've got no regrets. I had a nice job offer in Minneapolis once. More money, an office. But the guy who made me the offer had this smirky look on his face like he'd done me the biggest favor and he expected me to kiss his foot — Minneapolis! He was offering me *Minneapolis!* I looked him in the eye and said, 'No thanks, I'd rather stay where I am. Looseleaf, North Dakota. Good people.' Which was true. Leeds Cutter. There was a classy man. Practiced law here. Before your time. Had an office up over the bank. Sat up there and read books and sketched in his notepad and talked about everything except the law, talked about the Milky Way, the Civil War, bird migration, Duke Ellington, the secret of raising corn and soybeans, the breeding of cattle, everything interested him. I never saw him in a sour mood. He and Al and Deloyd and Charlie, we were all best friends. Started the Halloween parade back in 1938, you know. Everytime I saw those guys, it made me happy. No matter what else was going on, we always sat down and shot the bull and had some laughs. Never too busy to stop and talk. I tell you, that is a rare thing these days. So I have no regrets. You can't put a price on friendship, I say. No man is a failure who has friends."

"So what's your big hurry to leave?"

"It is what it is. This'll be my last Christmas. I can feel it. I'm on my way out, just like that African violet. A race to the finish. My mother took a long time, dying. She'd get close and we'd all gather around her bed and the old worry instinct kicked in and she started asking if we'd had supper and did we have colds and were we getting enough sleep and pretty soon she'd forgotten about dying and the next day she had to start all over. It's not recommended."

The old man was starting to nod now and Rosana was in the doorway, smiling, waiting to escort Uncle Earl to his nap. It was past noon. James stood up to go, though he didn't know where he was going. "See you tomorrow," he said.

"Good-bye. God bless you," said Rosana. Uncle Earl was dozing already.

"Want me to help get him to bed?"

"I'll get him there. I do it every day."

He touched the old man's forehead. "Thank you for everything," he whispered. Rosana reached down and picked up the bag with the liver and pancreas and put her other hand under Earl's left armpit. "Come on, old man," she said. "Come to bed, darling. Come, my love."

19. Leo's secret mission

He put the crusty old parka back on and a pair of insulated boots and lumbered out the back door and down the alley. The Methodist Men's Christmas tree lot had balsam firs and Scotch pine and spruce, and a sign said *Closed Pay What U Can* so he took a little spruce and stuck a hundred-dollar bill in the slot and put it over his shoulder. He stopped at Swedlund's Grocery and bought a bag of strong licorice, a package of Swedish meatballs, a bottle of chili sauce, a box of crackers. He didn't recognize the lady at the cash register. She said, "You're lucky, we close at noon." He was delaying going back to Floyd's shack for fear of what he might find there — open the door and walk into what? A concert hall where he'd have to sing his aria from *Messiah?* A hockey arena and he'd be the goalie on the losing side? He stepped into Phil's Happy Hour for a bottle of cognac. The bartender was tall with loose skin, like he'd just lost a hundred pounds or so. It wasn't early afternoon and men sat at the bar drinking their beer with shots of whiskey and watching an electric Santa in dark glasses play a guitar and sing, "I Yust Go Nuts For Christmas" and none of them seemed amused, though his belly shook like a bowlful of jelly and his guitar burst into flames. An old woman sat in a booth, a bottle of beer in front of her, three empty ones, and yelled into her cell phone, "You do exactly what you want to do because that's what you're going to do anyway, so there's no point in my arguing with you. I don't want anybody coming to my house for Christmas because they feel they have an obligation to. I would frankly rather spend Christmas alone with a frozen turkey dinner than be with people who don't enjoy my company."

The person at the other end tried to get in a word and she said, "No, no — that's fine — you made your choice, now stick with it. And merry Christmas." She snapped the cell phone shut and set it down on the table. It rang and she ignored it. The bartender searched under the bar and came up with a bottle of Armagnac. "Kinda steep," he said. "Forty bucks."

James gave him sixty. "That's for you. Merry Christmas."

The temperature had dropped to forty below zero. He noticed that -40 was as low as any thermometer in Looseleaf went — the little one attached to Earl's kitchen window, the big one beside the front door of the Westendorp Pure Oil station and the Cobb's Super Foods thermometer — evidently forty below zero was as much cold as anyone here cared to know about. But he was toasty warm in the big boots and balloon parka that had belonged to the late Floyd. He trudged along the path toward the lake and out onto the ice and got to Floyd's just as a snowmobile came buzzing alongside, and stopped, idling and sputtering, and it was Leo Wimmers. "Hey," he said. "I looked for you at Earl's and they said you'd come out here. Mind if I come in?" He stepped into Floyd's shack before he could be disinvited and took off his coat and sat down and James poured a couple fingers of Armagnac into a Dixie cup. And one finger into a second cup for himself. For mouthwash.

Leo was hot to talk: "Man's got to live his own life and not somebody else's. That's the dilemma. Floyd got trapped into Arizona. Tucson was Faye's idea, not his. He had nothing to do with it. She was gone most of the time, running around doing her Ojibway thing, talking up duality and global consciousness and so forth, and Floyd was left to wash the windows and water the lawn. But every January he managed to escape up here for a few weeks and sit in his fish house and enjoy the good life. He loved this old shack. He told me it was just like going to church except you didn't have to shake hands with people you don't like."

Leo took a seat by the fish hole and looked at the bobber in the water. "Liz is always after me to devote myself to the cause, but it isn't exactly my cause. That's the whole problem with marriage. Trying to maintain your course and not get sucked into the gravitational field of someone else. She says to me, 'Why don't you ever want to go to meetings with me?' She loves meetings. The Possum Comatosis. The Oak Tree Society. The Citizens For Life. You name it, she goes. Loves to go to town meetings organized by

Democrats and yell and wave signs. That's her. But it isn't me."

"I guess I always assumed you were more or less in her camp," James said. "I mean, you two met at a gun show — right?"

Leo nodded. "I never told anybody this, but I feel like I can trust you, seeing as you're with the C.I.A. and all. I was there at the gun show working undercover for the F.B.I. And I still am."

"You're with the F.B.I.?"

Leo closed his eyes. "You're the first person I told this to. It's been a real burden, but then that's in the nature of the work, and I knew that when I signed on for the mission."

"Who are you spying on, if I may ask?"

"Liz."

"The F.B.I. has you spying on your wife?"

Leo tossed back a swig of Armagnac. "She is plotting to overthrow the government of the United States. She and a couple hundred others. She's serious."

"And you're sleeping with her?"

"It isn't easy, believe me. But the only way I could get into her life undetected was for her to fall in love with me. So I seduced her. They have pharmaceuticals for that, you know. Hallucinogens. Two drops of it on a pretzel and she was climbing on my lap like a monkey."

"Fifteen years you've been sleeping with a suspect?"

"She's a very nice woman when she isn't all het up about conspiracies. We have a reasonably good marriage. Except I know that one day I will have to snap the cuffs on her and haul her in for trying to bring down the government. And that is painful, of course. The truth so often is."

"How exactly is she planning to do that?"

"Internet hacking. She's got sixteen guys working out of a basement room in the power plant. Your uncle's retired but he still runs the electric co-op and Liz has established a super-high-speed accelerated Internet center there that specializes in hacking into bank accounts and moving large sums of money around."

James looked at the little man in the big parka and wondered if a story was being spun here before his eyes. But the little man reached into his parka and opened up a Velcro pocket half-way down the left sleeve and pulled out a badge. Federal Bureau of Investigation. Special Agent.

And then the ice boomed, and Leo winced and got to his feet. "I'll fill you in on the rest later," he said, and exited, and the snowmobile engine revved and it buzzed away. It sounded like the cardboard James and Ralph used to fasten to their bike fenders to flap against the spokes and make a sort of engine sound. One summer they rode in and around Looseleaf with flaps buzzing and out the western road to the marsh and laid their bikes down in the tall grass and stripped and went in swimming, the skinny dark James, the skinny blonde Ralph. There was a crystal clear pool with lush lilypads in an inlet under overhanging cottonwoods and they lay around in there and thought out loud about various things —

Planes overhead: where are they going?

Do your parents have sex?

When will we die and what will happen then?

If you could be anyone in the world right now, who would it be?

What if a meteor hits the Earth and knocks it off orbit so that North Dakota becomes the tropics and the Caribbean is the new North Pole?

What if God told you to kill somebody, would you do it?

What if you had a million dollars?

The two of them were mostly agreed on basic principles: the planes were headed for California, carrying criminals and movie stars; parents did not have sex anymore — they had tried it once or twice and it didn't interest them; we will die when we are extremely old, like in our fifties; we would be either Clint Eastwood or Steve Cannon; if North Dakota became the tropics, it would be horrible and nobody could stand it; you would kill that person, but only if you were 100 percent sure; you would take your million dollars and put it in the bank at 3 percent interest and roam the world, Asia and South America, stay in ritzy hotels, eat steaks and ice cream, have a heckuva time.

It was from the shore near the pool by the cottonwoods that Ralph launched the canoe to go retrieve the dead ducks that October afternoon. He was 25 years old. Seventeen years ago.

He and James used to skate on their

long blades at this end of the lake, side by side, hands behind their backs, watchful of the spot off the end of the point where a spring bubbles up and the ice can be soft. People had gone through the ice there and in very cold weather, that would be the end of you, but they were two skating together so the other one would help the guy out of the slush and get him to shelter.

And Ralph saved his life once, out in the muskeg, north of there. Their scoutmaster Elmer took Troop 147 camping on the coldest night in January though some parents said, "What if one of the boys wanders away? He could die of exposure." Elmer said, "That will teach them to stick close together." They pitched a big canvas tent and built a bonfire and stood by the blaze, their front sides burning hot and their backsides freezing, and Elmer told the inspiring story of the Scoutmaster who rescued a boy who broke through the ice into the freezing water and saved him from hypothermia by stripping off his clothes and lying naked in a sleeping bag with him, warming him with the heat of his own body, which seemed extremely weird to the boys, and then they crawled into their sleeping bags and flopped down together in a big heap like sled dogs and slept, while keeping one eye open for Elmer.

James woke up in the middle of the night, in bluish moonlight, his breath billowing in the air, his bladder full and almost bursting, and he humped out through the flaps and was about to unzip and pee in the snowbank but then thought of Elmer's story and was afraid and trundled over the ridge and down a ravine and through a grove of birches to where Elmer couldn't see him — and pulled out his thing and the piss blew out of him with tremendous force, making an arc twelve feet long, steaming hot when it came out and when it hit the ground, it was a stream of ice chips that dinged like coins on the ground. He wrote in the snow, "Theresa, I love you" and then imagined the ice making its way up the arc toward the source of the stream and promptly stopped and zipped up, and then couldn't remember the way back to the tent. His tracks were not discernible on the hard crusted snow. The landmarks were unfamiliar. He climbed to the top of the ridge and saw no lights at all. And then he saw a steel pole sticking up out of the snow.

A surveyor's rod. And a voice in his head said, *You are going to walk over and put your tongue on it and there is absolutely nothing you can do to prevent this.*

He cried at the thought of his imminent death. The tears froze on his cheeks. The voice said, *Why wait? Why postpone the inevitable? Put your tongue on the rod. You know in your heart you will do it and you are right, you will. Do it now.* He thought of his weeping mother following the long pine box carried over the frozen ground by six townsmen in heavy parkas and his own body riding inside, in the cheap satin plush, and the preacher hurrying the prayer of commitment, his teeth chattering, and then the coffin falling slowly down into the depths of the frozen earth, and then a hand touched his shoulder and he jumped six feet and turned and it was Ralph. "You better come back," he said. James followed him up the ravine. "Why did you write my girlfriend's name in the snow?" he said. "That's a different Theresa," said James, lying. "You don't know her. She's not from here."

"That better be the truth," said Ralph.

And now Ralph had returned in the form of a gray wolf to give James the benefit of his insight. An amazing fact but then the world is full of them.

20. In the Coyote Coffee Shop on Parnassus Avenue, he meets his wise man

He stepped out on the ice and walked around back of the shack to take a leak and for the *n*th time was stunned by the beauty of the fresh snow, the frozen lake shining, cold and beautiful. And thought of his own death. He had come into the world around Christmastime and maybe he'd be leaving it too, to satisfy nature's craving for symmetry. The world would exist without him in it. The Coyote Corp. would get absorbed by some other nutrient conglomerate and vanish and his radio stations would go on yakking about horse hockey and Mrs. Sparrow would go on going to plays and nothing much would change. Mortality. It's in the back of your mind, but once you're aware of it back there, it moves to the front.

And then a light tap-tap-tap-tap on the door. Someone inside Floyd's shack, inviting him in. A strange sound. People around here knock three times — *knock knock knock.* Or some people knock five — *knock knock knock knock knock.*

This was four: *taptaptaptap.*

He zipped up and kicked clean snow on top of the yellow snow and walked around the shack and opened the door and walked into a coffee shop where a young man with a prominent beak and big eyebrows and a shaved head stood at the counter, the espresso machines behind him, and a cap on his head that said *Coyote Coffee.* The room was full of customers perusing newspapers or tapping away at laptops, young women in black, young men in billboard T-shirts, not a parka or pair of mittens in sight. An Asian man stood looking at the pastries, he wore a shirt with the Golden Gate bridge painted on the back. He smelled of a rich fragrance James had never encountered before.

The man behind the counter said, "May I help you?" and James said, "Where am I?"

"Parnassus Street. The Inner Sunset. San Francisco."

"Aha. Then I'll have a large latte with an extra shot. And a biscotti."

"For here, or to go?"

Well, that was a very good question.

But not one he could answer. On the other hand, why would a person buy a latte on Parnassus Street in San Francisco and take it out onto a frozen lake in North Dakota?

"For here," he said.

He knew without looking that he would not have money in his pocket — *of course* he would not have money in his pocket — that is in the nature of fables. The pocket is empty. Money buys you nothing here. All is fate and magic. And when the latte was made and the tall cup and the biscotti set down on the counter and he had explained to the coffee man that he was extremely sorry but he had no money on him, he had left home without it — the man grinned and said, "You're very funny, Mr. Sparrow. You own this place. Coffee's on the house."

He carried his coffee to the one empty seat in the café, at a table in the window where an old Chinese man sat dozing over his newspaper.

"Is this seat taken?" The Chinese man opened his eyes and gestured for him to sit down.

Outdoors, a trolley swung around the corner screeching and a woman pushed a stroller past with four sleeping babies in it, a full load.

"Pardon me," said Mr. Sparrow, "but I don't have much time. Twenty-four hours, in fact, and it's almost up, and this being a fable — and I think I know how fables work — you're supposed to speak some sort of wisdom to me. I mean, it's pretty obvious — one seat open in the whole café — and so maybe we could get right to it and if there's something more I need to do to win a reprieve, then I'll have time to do it. Okay?"

The old Chinese man looked at him and blinked. "Sparrow?" he said.

"Sparrow."

He reached into his pocket for a looseleaf notebook and paged through it slowly, looking at each sheet on which he had written dense lines of script in a fountain-pen hand. "Is this about sins of the flesh? Minnesota?"

"No, no, no — I'm from Chicago. I'm the guy who used to not like Christmas and then I was given twenty-four hours to get straightened out and my cousin Liz chopped a hole in the ice and I jumped in and it sort of unblocked things for me — anyway, the name is Sparrow. S-p-a-r-r-o-w."

"Oh. *Sparrow.* Yes. Mr. Sparrow."

The old Chinese man peered at him

closely and poured hot water into a tea cup and then flinched — he'd spilled some on his leg. James wasn't sure that a wise man in a fable should be doing that sort of thing, but he waited.

"This morning I saw a sparrow in a tree, a variety of sparrow I've never seen before. A blue-billed one. He looked at me with a cocked eye and I waited and waited and finally he flew up and dropped a slip of paper at my feet, a message meant for you. It says, 'Today you will be very lucky with the number three if you wait at the trolley stop where the lady with the red parasol spoke to you about your brother Frank."

"I have no brother Frank. My name is Sparrow. James Sparrow."

The man dropped a teabag in the

hot water. "James Sparrow?" James nodded.

"Ah yes. Very good. Very very good." The old Chinese man closed his eyes again and leaned his head back against the wall and seemed to snooze for a minute and James was about to nudge his foot and then the old man said softly, "I am in touch with the one who rules your fate, whatever you wish to call her."

James felt his heart clench and the room seemed to inhale and contract. He felt a coronary occlusion coming on and in two seconds he'd pitch forward onto the floor and lie there, trying to draw breath.

And then his phone rang. It was Mrs. Sparrow.

"Darling? How are you?"

"I'm fine. Enjoying a heckuva

snowstorm."

"How's Uncle Earl?"

"He got himself an attractive Indian caregiver and now he's sitting up and taking nourishment. Listen, sweetheart —"

"How soon do you think you can leave?"

"Airport's still snowed in, darling. How's your flu? Did you go see the doctor about it?"

"I did and he says I'll be fine."

"Good. Darling, if you don't mind —"

"I called to ask you a really big favor, if you'd be able to come back here and let's go to Hawaii together."

"Of course."

"I miss you."

"I miss you."

"I mean, I miss you terribly. Would

you mind?"

"No problem."

"You'd tell me if it was, wouldn't you?"

"It's not."

"I know, but you'd tell me if it was, right?"

"Darling —"

"You're the most giving and generous person I know."

"May I call you back in an hour?"

"You're busy, aren't you."

"It's all right."

"Listen, I'm sorry I bothered you."

"Darling, I'll come back for you. I just need to figure something out."

"I'm probably interrupting something. You're probably in the middle of a meeting right now."

"I am, but it's okay."

"Oh my God. I'm sorry."

"I'll call you back —" Another trolley came rolling by.

"Where are you? What's that bell clanging?"

"It's a long story. Later." He clicked off the phone.

The old Chinese man said, "You are a lucky man, Mr. Sparrow. You almost married Theresa Donderewicz and that would have been a terrible mistake. It was December. You were nineteen years old and desperate to be loved and she seemed willing and you went for a walk at night and wound up in the cemetery and you lied to her about how you planned to go to law school and the truth was, you'd been kicked out of college for extreme nonattendance, but you told her you'd take her to Paris. You didn't know how desperate she was. She went to

Fargo and planned to sing and dance and amaze people but found out she wasn't at all amazing in Fargo, only adequate, that Looseleafers cannot astonish in Fargo, so she cried for three nights, standing under a stoplight, hoping to be discovered by someone special, then went home and saw you. You seemed like a live possibility. So she invited you home and took you into the basement and you two sat on a bed and kissed for a while, and took each other's clothes off and were just about to intertwine and then the basement door opened and her father called her name and she answered. You hid in the corner. He came down the stairs and saw her lying under a blanket and she told him she couldn't sleep in her own bed because it was too warm upstairs so she came down there, and then he saw your shoes and your pants. He cursed and went galloping upstairs to get a gun and you snatched up your clothes and ran out the back way, naked on a bitter cold night, and made it to Uncle Earl's and he took mercy on you. He told Mr. Donderewicz that you'd been sitting in his kitchen playing pinochle and he described the game in great detail and Mr. Donderewicz, though suspicious, went snarling away, and your life was saved. Had you done what you intended to do, you'd be driving a truck of liquid nitrogen and enduring your father-in-law's rages."

James remembered Theresa. How desperate he was that winter. He'd come home broke and disheartened and worked shoveling sidewalks, and lived in his parents' attic for a month, and every morning Daddy asked him, "When are you going to do something with yourself?" And he didn't know.

"There were numerous occasions when you almost ran off the tracks," said the old man. "I could go down the list if you like. You applied for a job at Radio City Music Hall on that trip to New York when you were 26 and so starstruck by New York and the Rockettes and the Christmas show and the tap-dancing Santas. It was a production assistant job and they passed you over for a guy with a B.A. from Princeton and now he's running a road show of 'Walden: The Musical' on the junior college circuit and heavily medicated. And the slip of paper from the drunken chemist — you almost sold that to your marketing man for a hundred grand. You were in debt and you'd met Joyce and gone to Mackinac Island with her and the offer sounded good to you. And you asked her and she said absolutely no."

James had forgotten that and now it came back: their little apartment in Ravenswood, the kitchen with the yellow table, the Monet water lilies poster on the wall, a late night, the two of them sitting with two glasses of Rioja and a block of cheddar and some chips, and the soon-to-be-Mrs.-Sparrow telling him that 4xPrime was the next new thing and he should hang onto it for dear life and ride it for all it was worth.

The old man had found his voice now and he leaned across the table and spoke to James with quiet conviction.

"You are the benefactor of great kindness. And you have no idea how much goodness is lavished on the world by invisible hands. Small selfless deeds engender tremendous force against the darker powers. Great kindness pervades this world, struggling against pernicious selfishness and vulgar narcissism and the vicious streak that is smeared across each human heart — great bounding goodness is rampant and none of it is wasted. No, these small gifts of goodness — this is what saves the soul of man from despair, and that is what preserves humanity from the long fall from the precipice into the abyss."

So his dream — his habitual nightmare of being hunted in tall grass and attempting to escape and only edging closer to the precipice overlooking the dark abyss, the sharks, the big black birds, etc.

"Yes," said the old Chinese man. "This is not a prophetic dream, it is a revelation of how you have been brought safely over dangerous shoals and through narrow passages unawares. And now your trip to Looseleaf has resulted in much good. You have cheered up your uncle who was descending toward death and is now having a last encore of pleasure before he leaves."

"When will he die?" said James.

"Tuesday. And you made peace with your cousin whom you dislike, and you fought your other cousin to a draw and that was good for her soul, to be withstood. She's had it all her way for most of her life and now there's a little hole in her roof and she can view the sky. Any way you can offer a fellow being a new prospect is a kindness.

"But the loveliest was your twenty-dollar tip for Myrt, who was embarrassed by the generosity and meant to run after you and give it back but the truth is, she is short on cash and there is nothing shameful about need nor about what satisfies it. We give and we take. She takes your money which she needs to buy a Frank Sinatra CD, *Songs for Lovers,* and a pack of Camels and a bottle of beer for her old aunt Lois who needs to feel twenty-six again and dancing at the Spanish Gardens ballroom in Santa Barbara with Jack McCloskey the textile salesman and her first true love the night they necked in his pink convertible with the night breeze rich with eucalyptus and palm and though she knew he was not long for her arms, still he was gentle and sweet to her and told her he loved her over and over as he made love to her, which, at twenty-six, she had never experienced before, and so this was a revelation that despite the sarcasm of her sisters and the harsh remarks of her mother, Lois could be loved, and now, years later, listening to Mr. Sinatra and smoking a cigarette in her upstairs bedroom, she will call up Jack who is seventy-eight years old and in poor health in a care center in Provo, Utah, which Myrt located via the Internet, and Aunt Lois will tell Jack McCloskey that the memory of that January night remains a lamp in her heart, and this kind word, after years of sodden despair, will illuminate his night and move him to finally and absolutely sign over his wealth to the Jeremiah Program for single mothers, and thereby vast goodness will be achieved."

The old Chinese man smiled for the first time in his monologue. "So you see what you've done, Mr. Sparrow. More than you know."

"What about Christmas?"

"What about it? It's a nice day. Take a long walk. Sing more and talk less. Try putting ginger in the cranberry. It helps."

21. Christmas Eve arrives

He walked out of Coyote Coffee and onto the ice, San Francisco gone, but it had stopped snowing. He could hear distant snowplows scraping the pavement. Maybe the airport would get cleared today but he wasn't ready to go. It was noon in North Dakota and he was bone tired and lay down and slept in the fish house for a few hours and awoke in the cold and pulled on his boots and walked toward town. It was perfectly quiet, the countryside covered with snowdrifts, and he could hear everything that was happening and nothing was happening. No doors slammed, no car started, nobody yelling. He passed the Bon Ton Café and Myrt waved to him gaily. Rosana let him in to Uncle Earl's and shushed him — the old man was napping — and James lay down on the couch and fell asleep to the fish tank bubbler, and then suddenly it was Christmas Eve and everyone was there and the room was full of candles, bayberry, cranberry — "You'd think we were Catholic!" said Liz — and the old man was decked out in red pants and a white shirt with light-up bowtie and a red clown nose and a red headband with a small spring arm that held a sprig of mistletoe over his old white head. He was holding the bag with his liver and pancreas in a plastic flowerpot that played "In The Mood," a gift from a grandchild. He said, "Boy. Time sure flies, doesn't it. Got this flowerpot in 1997. Seems like only yesterday."

Faye wore a long white gown and sequins in her hair and a crown of holly and electric candles and served saffron buns and coffee. She had brought a centerpiece made from an egg carton and green garbage bag twists, very glittery, pictures of shepherds and angels and Democrats, FDR and JFK and MLK and BHO. Liz glanced at it without comment. Oscar arrived with a great fury of stamping and shaking snow off his pants and walked in, the prodigal brother who wasn't speaking to anybody, and all was forgiven — Liz hugged him and said the cologne he was wearing smelled more like disinfectant and if he had an infection she wanted to know about it. "That's the cologne you gave me three years ago, called Christmas Charisma. First time I put some on," he said and he took a cup of coffee and poured cream and sugar in it and sat on a hassock and told James he was looking good. Rosana appeared with a big red stocking for James with a dozen multi-colored pens and Post-its and candy and a giant navel orange.

Faye had bought Christmas gifts for everyone, porcelain trivets from Peru and hand-knitted tea cosies from Costa Rica. "These are made by peasants who were paid a fair wage for them," she said. Everyone examined their trivet, which had paintings of stick people doing things with animals. Liz had brought copies of a book called *Alien Reptiles* by Ann

Coulter, arguing that life-forms from outer space had taken over Washington.

The gifts were wrapped in a big hurry, you could see that — paper scrunched, tape slapped on, no ribbons, no bows — par for the course in these busy times — but he remembered Joyce and how she believed in beautiful wrapping. What's important is not the cash value of the gift but the loving intention of the giver — and you show this by how the gift — even the $1.69 bottle of Swank cologne — is wrapped. The recipient holds this work of art in his hands and notices how perfectly the ribbon is placed and the bow is handmade, and the paper is precisely folded into thin trapezoids at the ends, no creases, no wrinkles, and the perfection of the package serves to delay the opening of the gift, which prolongs anticipation, which heightens pleasure.

Joyce had elegance in her soul. She grew up nerdy, tomboyish, awkward, and she learned elegance from the inside out, which is the only way. She spoke elegantly. She carried herself with grace even back when she had little disposable income, there was a rightness about her that he meant to cherish now that his eyes had been opened by the dive into freezing water.

"What are these little crisp round things?" said Liz, pawing through the appetizers.

"Fried pig brains," said Oscar. "They're good. Try one."

"I requested them," said Uncle Earl. "The condemned man gets to choose.

I've loved pig brains since I was just a little squirt."

And just then, Leo, who never did this sort of thing, spread his arms and sang, "Hail hail the gang's all here" in his quavery tenor and flung a handful of sparkle dust over them. He gave James a big hug and whispered, "I'm planning to make my move and I may need your help." *What a Judas.* James brushed him away. "Not now," he said. "I've got enough on my plate as it is."

Oscar said, "I remember the time that busload of psychoanalysts got stranded here in December. What year was that? They were going to a convention in Vancouver and took the bus because they were afraid to fly. It was a snowy night and the bus rolled into town and stopped to use the men's room at the Bon Ton and that took a couple hours because there was just one stall and they all had to do Number 2 and each of them had his little ceremonies and reading material and so forth, and by the time they were done, the roads were drifted over and we had to put them up for the night. Actually, for three days. Forty-five short bald men with beards. I remember they loved macaroni noodles in mushroom soup sauce and canned tuna and peas. We took them ice fishing, and they loved that. It was a great novelty to them, sitting in a dark house and looking at a hole in the ice with a fish-line hanging down and a bobber floating in the water. They sat for hours, watching the bobber, writing in their little notebooks. They were sad to leave, I remember. Got on the bus and put their faces to the windows and waved their hankies and away they went."

"That was in fifty-eight," said Uncle Earl. "I remember. It was the year I went to Rapid City for the Rural Electrification convention."

"Nope. Eighty-five," said Oscar. "I remember it because eighty-five was when Sandy ran away with the extension agent."

"She didn't exactly run away," said Liz. "She only went as far as Fargo."

"She went far enough," said Oscar, "but anyway, that's all water under the bridge. Eighty-five. That was a hard winter. We had to eat the cat that year. You ever eat cat? They are not as meaty as they look. It was like pork except tough. I don't think it's anything that is going to catch on, if you know what I mean. That winter we had to bust up the dining room table for firewood and you know something? Mahogany does not burn well. Mostly it just smoldered. We got a bad case of head lice that winter and Aunt Cooter went berserk. Remember that? She was running from room to room, crying out about seeing Jesus up on high and trying to take her clothes off — she was yelling, 'I want to put on the *new* raiment! Put away this old raiment, put on the *new* raiment!' Boy, that got tiresome real fast. We kept wrapping her up in sheets and she kept ripping them off. She'd been weak and puny for years but suddenly she had strength in her arms. It happens when people go berserk. I read that somewhere. We just ran out of patience. We threatened to put her in the loony bin but she was seeing Jesus so it didn't matter to her. Finally we had to give her a tranquilizer and I guess we overtranquilized her because she died. But she went quietly in her sleep, which was how she always wanted to go. And she saw Jesus, so that must have been a comfort. It was too cold to bury her right away, the ground was frozen so hard. They were going to use dynamite but the families of other dead people objected to that, so we just put her in the tool shed until spring. Stood her up and leaned her against the lumber pile."

"I was in Arizona that winter," said Faye and started to launch into a story about the Hopi, but Oscar went on.

"That was the winter I went out to check my wolf traps and I slipped and fell on a patch of ice in the driveway. I'd plugged in the car to keep it thawed out and it was too cold and the radiator burst and the antifreeze froze. That's how cold it was. Anyway, I fell wrong and broke my leg and the bone poked right out through my pantleg. Luckily it was so cold I couldn't feel a thing. Well, I picked up some ice chunks and tossed them at the kitchen window and finally Rocky came and saw me. He was eight. I motioned for him to come help me and pointed to the protruding bone and finally he came out and stood on the back step. I said, 'Honey, I need you to go in the house and call the ambulance. If you don't, Daddy will freeze to death. Okay?' "

"He said, 'Why did you call me "Honey"? You never called me "Honey" before.' "

"I said, 'I called you Honey because I love you. You're my son and I love you dearly.'"

"He said, 'Why didn't you ever say so before?'"

"I said, 'Because I didn't want you to get the big head.'"

"He said, 'Before I call the ambulance, is it okay if I watch TV for an hour?'"

"I said, 'If you do that, Daddy will freeze to death and you'll feel just awful.'"

"He said, 'Oh.' And then he asked how much money I'd give him to call the ambulance. I offered him candy. He said he'd prefer money. He went to get the checkbook and he brought it out to me. I was going to grab his leg and get him down on the ground and wallop him but he tossed me the checkbook and a pen and told me to write it out for six thousand dollars. And I would've done it but just then, the wolf came around the garage and sat down and looked at me. I told Rocky to go in the house and get the gun. And then I thought better of it. I told him to go get the package of sirloins out of the freezer. So he did. He tossed it to the wolf. The wolf tried to chew his way into it but it was hard as a board. And there I lay, all fresh and meaty. Luckily, Sandy came home right at that moment. She ran the wolf off with a rake and then she told me that four thousand dollars would be enough for her, so I wrote out the check and the ambulance came and I was in the hospital for three weeks, and the leg's been fine, except it throbs whenever a storm is on the way."

James asked why Oscar was trapping for wolves and he said there had been a wolf who frightened some children and was coming too close to town and Faye and James glanced at each other.

They sat chewing their food thoughtfully and Liz said, "I never heard that story before."

Oscar said, "That's because I never told it before."

"Where is Rocky now?" said Faye.

Oscar didn't know. They hadn't heard from him since he got out of the Navy and got a job in New York driving a double-decker London omnibus.

"I remember waiting for the schoolbus when I was a kid," said James and was just about to launch into a story about that, but Uncle Earl jumped in and talked about the winter of 1931. "There never was a winter like it. Snow blew into big drifts a hundred feet high, like mountains, and though it was only ten miles to school, they sent Mr. Turner to pick us up in his sleigh. He wore a big fur cap and had eyebrows the size of rats and a big handlebar mustache, and he drove a team of black horses pulling a sleigh with a bearskin rug with the head of the bear still attached and us youngens dove under the bearskin and Mr. Turner cracked the whip and off we went to school. We crossed the river over the ice and rode through the swamp and were attacked there by ragged men in gray who leaped out from behind stumps, the last desperate remnants of the Army of Northern

Virginia looking for little Yankee children to kidnap for ransom in hopes of raising money to buy gunpowder from the Canadians and put the Confederacy together again. Old men in gray waving their rifles and whooping and yelling, and we had to race away across the frozen tundra and get to school, which was held in a cave back then. You crawled in through a long narrow hole to a cavern where you could stand up, and there were flaming torches set in iron brackets in the stones, and deep down below the earth, there was an enormous room heated by hot springs that bubbled up in a pool, and dazzling bright because the walls were quartz and jasper and mica which reflected the lantern light and made it feel like sunlight, and acres of precious stones lying loose all around, and we sat down at our desks feeling warm and happy and I don't know where our teachers came from — children didn't ask so many questions back then, we were brought up to accept things as they were and be grateful and not ask why — but they were very beautiful women with long golden hair in soft tendrils who circulated among us singing in low voices and their feet were bare and did not quite touch the ground. We were so grateful to be safe from the blizzard, we did our lessons faithfully and learned how to spell, which children today who grow up with reliable electrical power, and computers, never learn. Their spelling is atrocious. No reason not to love them, of course. They are wonderful kids. But I just wonder sometimes."

Twelve people around the long table, and out came a crock of fish soup redolent of onion and garlic and platters of meat and potatoes and a boatload of gravy and Uncle Earl arose to say grace, holding his internal organs in his hand. "This is my last Christmas, Lord, and I am fully grateful for it. Thank you for bringing me this far. I ask no more. Thank you for Rosana and thanks to Jefferson County for the generosity. And thank you, Lord, for this brief time of peace and contentment and everybody getting along. And now let's eat." Rosana stood in the doorway, dabbing at her eyes. "Dig in!" he hollered. They sat and chewed and the sheer butteriness of everything, the turkey and gravy, the glitter of fat in the spuds, made them dozy, and then Liz, who had had three glasses of red wine, clinked on her glass and stood up and said, "I'm glad you're all having fun and I hope that in the midst of it all, you stop to consider that this may well be our last Christmas in a free country unless people listen to the truth and take action. But I promised Leo I wasn't going to talk politics on Christmas so I won't. I want to thank you, Daddy, for making me feel good about myself and not have to be like everybody else. And when you're gone, I'm going to stay here in Looseleaf and build a community of people dedicated to freedom." And she plopped down.

Well, Faye was not about to let Liz hog the spotlight, so she popped right up and spread her hands out in a long lingering beneficent gesture, her eyes closed, and said, "This is a thank you to the force of love that watches over all of us now and at all times, without which we would be lost forever."

"Oh god," said Liz.

Faye was unfazed. "In the great Ojibway tradition and in the traditions of all of us in the storytelling community, this time of year is sacred because it is a time of going back to origins and first causes, and whether we tell the story of the Christ-child come to earth in Bethlehem and surrounded by cattle and shepherds, or we tell the story of the Great White Bear who led our ancestors over the ice bridge from Siberia and down into the New World, this is nonetheless a sacred time and a time when each of us can pause and recollect our own story of who we are and where we come from and in this way get a clearer visualization of our journey —"

Oscar dinged on his glass. "Excuse me but your ancestors didn't come over on an ice bridge from Siberia, they came from England on a ship. You're English, same as us. You're not Ojibway."

"I was made Ojibway in a spirit healing ceremony on the Arizona desert six years ago," she said. "I was born again on the desert, holding the sacred yucca in my hands, smoking the sacred mesquite."

"You've been smoking too much mesquite, then," he said. "You're one of us, Faye. Indian you ain't."

"Don't limit other people, Oscar. I'm a traveler. I am not defined by your opinion of me."

"Not defining you, Faye. Just telling you who you are so you don't make a fool of yourself."

Uncle Earl got to his feet and dinged on a glass for silence. "I just remembered more about 1931. I was just a kid. I knew we didn't have much money. Our clothes were thin and we ate bean soup twice a day and I gave Mama all the money from my paper route, but nonetheless she wanted to have Christmas. She went to the store and bought a big orange for me and a book, *The Chilstrom Boys On the S.S. Araby,* about two farm boys who stow aboard a freighter for the South Seas and solve the robbery of a sacred jade. We had beeswax candles and she lit them and we waited for Dad to come home from the farm where he was hiring out to muck out the barn for an old lady. He had to walk five miles to get home and it was late when he arrived, all worn out and discouraged, and Mama waiting up for him with two cups of eggnog and a shot of bourbon and two cigarettes. They were staunch Methodists but on Christmas Eve they made an exception. So they smoked a cigarette and sipped the eggnog and she put on the radio, and a jazz band was playing, and she danced with him. But his heart wasn't in it. She put his hand on her thigh and tried to kiss him but he turned away. My mother and dad standing on an old linoleum floor in candlelight and the old Atwater-Kent turned up and a man was singing about a cottage for two, and her trying to kiss him and him turning away. It broke her heart. They thought I was asleep but I wasn't. She sat down and smoked that second cigarette alone and he looked out the window. He said, 'We can't afford to have another baby now. Can't even afford the one we got.' And she said, 'I'm not talking about that.' And he said nothing, and she said, 'I'm taking Buddy and going to live with my sister in North Dakota.' And that's how I came here."

Rosana brought out bowls of walnuts and dates and a pitcher of eggnog with rum to flavor it, and Ozzie sat down at the piano and banged out *"On The Road to Mandalay / where the flying fishes play / and the dawn comes up like thunder / out of China cross the bay"* and *"Nita Juanita, tell my soul that we must part . . . Nita Juanita, lead thou on, my heart"* — they stood shoulder to shoulder behind Ozzie, their voices mingling, coming with all the faithful upon a midnight clear to see the radiant streams from Thy holy face. And then Uncle Earl started singing "Silent Night" and Faye turned out the lights and the candles flickered, the fragrance of pine in the air, and coffee and saffron, and outside the snow was falling and James, who hadn't cried real tears since last Christmas, could feel them coming around again.

Everyone was in a mellow mood, even Liz.

Uncle Earl opened up a fresh bottle of brandy. "Clean glasses!" he said to Faye and she jumped up and got a box of Dixie cups. "Glasses!" he said. "The good ones!" So she rustled up the family heirloom Waterford crystal goblets and washed the dust off and Earl poured a couple fingers of brandy in each and swished some around in his mouth and leaned back and closed his eyes. James stood in front of him, a camera in hand, and shot pictures of the old man, his eyes closed, as any storyteller does when delving deep into memory.

"I remember the year I went up to Alaska to drive truck when they were building the Alcan Highway and I stuck around in November to go bear hunting with some Eskimos I met in a bar in Fairbanks and that was the year a storm came through on Armistice Day and dumped about six feet of snow. Well, we just stayed with the truck and got out okay, but we heard about a mining camp just south of there — they hadn't gotten their provisions in, and when two weeks passed and no help arrived, they looked around at each other and made some difficult choices. They scratched off the bonier ones — too hard to clean — and they marked a couple of the fat ones for harvesting. And of course the fat men knew it, even though the others tried to pretend it wasn't happening — 'Huh? What shotgun? Is this a shotgun? Oh. This shotgun. Well, I don't know how it got here.' And late at night, after devotions, the two fat men made their escape. They snuck out and put on their snowshoes and headed for the highway. Two great big guys. One was the camp cook and the other was the dynamiter who set off the charges in the mineshaft when they needed to go deeper. Well, being hefty men and no athletes, they got winded after a couple thousand yards, and the alarm bell rang, and the camp organized a rescue party to go find them. A hunting party, I should say. The moon was full and the fat men's trail was easy to follow, the way they thrashed around in the snow, and the hunters spotted them making their way around the south face of Golden Girl Mountain and saw how slow they were moving. So the hunters circled down to the lower slopes to intercept them at a line of aspen trees. They'd shoot both of them right there, gut them, skin them, butcher the meat, and pack it out on a toboggan. Easy pickings. They hid in the aspens, licking their chops, waiting for dinner to arrive, and then they saw a flash of flame. They knew what it was and tried to run but the snow was too deep. The dynamiter had set off a charge and started the biggest avalanche you ever saw. Half the mountain came sliding down and the two fat men rode down on it, paddling and kicking like crazy to stay afloat, and the hungry men in the aspen trees were never seen again. The fat men rode the snow for six miles all the way down to the Matanuska Valley and slid up to the highway just as a bus came along. It stopped. On the bus were fifteen attractive young ladies who were part of an evangelism crusade and ten lumberjacks who thought they'd died and gone to heaven. Fifteen women for ten men seemed like the right ratio to them, and of course the ladies were all born-again Christians, but — if only the bus would get stuck and all of them be snowbound for a week or two or three, the lumberjacks figured that human nature would take its course and the pleasure urge prevail. And then these two fatsos climb aboard all snowy and wet, and that promised to screw everything up. The lumberjacks bided their time until the bus came to a snowslide and stopped. It was twilight. The lumberjacks got out shovels to dig and the dynamiter spoke up nice and pert and said, 'Hey, I know a better way!' So he prepared a charge of dynamite. A couple big red sticks tied together and a long fuse and he got it all rigged up, the lumberjacks hoping he'd set it off accidentally and blow himself sky-high, and he laid it in the deepest part of the snowbank and hollered 'Fire in the hole!' and all the lumberjacks dashed for cover. But while the charge was being rigged, the cook had gone around and let air out of the bus tires and so he and the dynamiter jumped on board the bus with the girls and drove right over the snow-slide. And when the lumberjacks gave chase, the dynamite went off and the lumberjacks slid into a deep crevasse and it took ten days to rescue them by which time they'd gone berserk and were drooling and pulling out their hair by the fistful. Two men with fifteen young women who were praising God for their deliverance. The cook and the dynamiter had a day and a half to get to know the girls and when they got to Anchorage, each of them had found a wife, and of course they had to go to church and get saved but that was a small price to pay for the love of a beautiful woman."

And then Leo stood up. James looked up at the man and he thought Leo looked quite festive and jolly but no, that wasn't the case.

"This is the fifteenth Christmas I've spent with all of you here in Looseleaf and I want to thank you for all these wonderful stories of bygone days of yesteryear and now I have a little story of my own. But not so sweet."

Liz looked at him thoughtfully.

"Next week I am moving to Washington, D.C., to take up a new position in the anti-terrorism office of the F.B.I." He reached into his pocket and pulled out the badge. "My name isn't Wimmer, it's Krainis. Lawrence B. Krainis, Special Agent. I've been here undercover and now my job is done." He turned to Liz. "I just want you to know, from the heart, that you were everything I ever wanted in a wife. It's not about you at all."

Liz did not seem fazed whatsoever.

"If it's the Possum Comatosis you're after, G-Man, you're a day late and a dollar short."

He nodded. "I realize that. You're a step ahead of me, Liz."

"Three steps, G-Man. I knew somebody was watching us because I sense satellite waves and so I moved the Freedom Center out of the power plant last fall. Put them on a truck and wished them well and I have no idea where they went. But somewhere in America, they're working to re-establish the Constitution of the United States of America. You can count on that big time."

Leo — or Lawrence B. Krainis — shrugged. "I admit defeat. But you can't expect me to go back to my superiors empty-handed."

"You've got nothing on me,

G-Man."

Faye rose and grabbed a carving knife from beside the platter of turkey.

"If this is about the sacred medicinal plants of the Ojibway, you've bitten off more than you can chew, white man. I may talk like a hophead but I could put this knife between your ribs as easy as I could filet a walleye, maybe easier."

"Your drug habits don't interest me, Faye, and they're of no interest to the government. And neither are you. But bank robbery is." He turned to James. "Mitchell, Pierre, Rapid City, and Billings. Ring a bell?"

James faced him just like he'd faced the wolf. "I think you're barking in the wrong culvert, Mr. Krainis. It's Christmas and you're a guest here.

And no longer a welcome one."

The F.B.I. agent pulled a snub-nosed revolver out of his breast pocket and aimed it at James's chest. "There's no holiday where crime is concerned," he said. He walked slowly around the table, his eyes flitting from side to side lest anyone should attempt a sudden sneaky move. Oscar had jumped to his feet and Rosana had come into the room holding a whisk. "Nobody move so much as an eyebrow or this roscoe's gonna start talking," he said, as he sidled around Uncle Earl's chair, stepping onto the plastic bag containing the liver and the pancreas. The old man let out a shriek and the F.B.I. man jumped back. Uncle Earl clutched his abdomen. "I'm leaving!" he yelled. "I'm out of here! I got only seconds to live! Better come give me a hug right now and don't wait. The shades of night are falling fast! The curfew bell is a-ringing! I can hear them calling! It's the moaning of the bar! Heading out to sea! O yes — the end is nigh!" Liz knelt down by his side and Faye grabbed him, as the G-man backed toward the door. "No sudden moves," he said. "I've got you covered." Just as an old gray-haired lady in a black silk dress and a veil stepped smartly into the room and pulled out a pump handle and swung it and hit him right in the elbow, in that tender spot that everyone knows so well, and he dropped the revolver and grabbed his elbow and jumped up and down in pain, crying out *Oh oh oh oh oh oh oh*. His long training as an F.B.I. agent had not prepared him for the vulnerability of this particular bone.

Uncle Earl laughed to see it. Despite his bruised organs, the sight of the agent dancing in pain and emitting high-pitched squeals amused him, and he chortled and slapped his thigh. He said, “You were the most boring son-in-law a man could have, Leo, but I see you had terpsichorean talent we hadn’t known about. And now I’d be obliged if you’d just get in your car and drive away.”

“Can’t drive away. We’re snowbound,” said Mr. Krainis in a wounded voice.

The old woman in the doorway said, “You’re not snowbound anymore.” It was Joyce, dressed up as Mrs. Manicotti. She looked at James and gestured with her thumb. “You,” she said. “Come with me.”

She led him out the door and as they

left, there was a tremendous roar in the street and a burst of flame. Simon was there, fussing and all proprietary, and Ramon and Buzz and Buddy, holding onto the ropes of an enormous red-and-green hot air balloon, the basket balanced on the snow, and the pilot in it, pulling the lanyard that switched on the burner that heated the air inside the bag, which rose six stories in the air. "Where did you come from?" James said.

"I rode the North Coast Limited train," Joyce said. "This is the engineer." She pointed to the old Chinese man from the coffee shop. "The balloon was in the baggage car and it looks like we arrived just in time to save you from Leavenworth." She took off the gray wig and the black silk dress and under it was the green cashmere number he'd given her for Christmas three years before.

He helped her into the basket and climbed up behind her and Simon started to swing himself aboard and lost his grip and fell off into a snowbank ("Arghhh!") as the burner roared again and up they rose on Christmas Eve, the stars in the sky, exactly as you see on Christmas cards. Shimmery flakes fell through the air. A lovely night, the old streetlights sliding away beneath them and the lights of Christmas trees in houses, snowy branches on the bare trees, walkers out, even a jogger or two in Spandex outfits and face masks, looking up and waving as the balloon rose over the town. Headlights moved slowly on the streets of town and beyond, the highway lay under undulating swells of snow, a vast white blanket. The burner blasted another long blast of flame and then silence as they floated over the gray treelines, the lights in the windows of the barns and farmhouses twinkling for miles around. Up above, nebulae spiraling in the winter sky, and all around them the chill pristine beauty of the world of stillness. "Heading south-southeast," said the pilot. "Should make Fargo around two in the morning. Roads are clear in Fargo, the airport is open. We'll get you on a 6 A.M. flight to Minneapolis and you should be in Chicago by noon." The burner blasted again. "Better go below and stay warm," he said, and they crawled down below the deck and into a warm nest of down blankets and lay in each other's arms.

"I have news," she said.

"I figured it out," he said.

"I'm expecting a baby."

"That's wonderful."

"You're not upset?"

"I'm happy as I can be."

The rigging groaned as a gust of wind caught the balloon and then the burner roared and they rose with a whoosh.

She fell asleep in the rocking of the basket and he snaked his hand under the woolen blanket and into her dress and onto her bare belly. It was firm and he thought he could feel something tremble. Inside slept his child, so newly formed it was neither boy nor girl yet, just a seed showing a sort of head and tail, but pushing harder toward completion, an entire person.

Epilogue

When Mr. Sparrow got back home to the Wabasha Tower from a blissful week with Mrs. Sparrow floating in the warm salt sea, he told Simon to find him a homeless man who was his, James's, size and buy him several winter outfits (and spring ensembles) from a good store and bring the old clothes back to James.

"If this is a test and the correct answer is, No, I won't," said Simon, "then No, I won't."

But he returned a few hours later with a green garbage bag full of filthy disgusting rags and a video of the previous owner, a gaunt toothless man named Roy Ypsilanti standing in the doorway of Nieman-Marcus in a new down coat, black wool trousers, a fur Cossack cap in his hands, which he clutched like a trophy. He smiled a sweet gummy grin and said, "Thank you, Mr. Sparrow. You are a gentleman and a Christian." And teared up. James turned the TV off.

"I don't know what you're going to do with the clothing," said Simon. "But at least let me wash it." He opened the green bag. It stank.

"Washing it would obviate the point." James pulled his shirt off over his head and then dropped his trousers. He pulled on a pair of tan corduroys that smelled of rot and excrement. The zipper was gone, the fly closed with a strip of duct tape, and the waist tied with a length of clothesline. He pulled on a crusty sweatshirt and a sweater, and a torn plastic poncho, and looked at Simon and grinned. "Who am I now?"

"If you need a personal reference, I'm here to help."

He put on the man's busted black leather shoes and picked up the garbage bag and said, "Checkbook." Simon handed him the tan leather-bound checkbook.

He boarded the service elevator and descended to the garage — the elevator stopped on the 14th floor and a woman stepped in and then quickly stepped out — and in the garage he walked down the aisle of cars and past his red Audi convertible and up the ramp — the electric eye flashed and the big door opened — and up into the cold January morning he went, around the corner past the wine store and the Café Monet and down the street to St. Ansgar's.

He went to four churches that Sunday morning and in the first one, three ushers gently took him by the collar and ushered him out the door and one got on a cell phone and called for reinforcements while another told James where he could find a homeless shelter. "It's six blocks away, you can't miss it," he said. "I was hungry and you gave me food, I was naked and you gave me raiment," said James. "Exactly," said the man. "That's what they do there."

In the second church, he was allowed to sit in a rear pew but was closely watched by two men alongside him and one up front. A family sitting in the pew in front of him got up and moved. The minister in the pulpit kept glancing James's way uneasily, as if a dog had wandered in.

In the third church, a man invited him to come downstairs and join a discussion group that was meeting to talk about homelessness. "I came to worship," said James. The man said he thought James would find the discussion group more up his line.

Finally, in the fourth church, a woman in a white cassock and silvery cape smiled at him and reached for his hand and said, "Welcome. We're so glad to see you. We are happy you joined us for worship today." And meant it. It happened to be St. Giles Cathedral, a big stone Gothic pile with a choir in fancy robes and starched collars, but they were genuinely friendly so he pulled out his checkbook and wrote the church a check for a stupendous amount of money and handed it to the smiling woman and said, "That's for real. Not a joke." She did not look at the check but put it in the collection plate in a mess of tens and twenties, which she placed on the table behind her and said, "I love your 4xPrime. Couldn't live without it. And I had a dream about you last night, Mr. Sparrow. I dreamed that you were on our Christmas Committee."

"It'd be my pleasure," he said, and it really was his pleasure, and he is still on the Christmas Committee twelve years later, organizing the annual Christmas Dance and pouring the excellent cranberry punch and teaching people how to do the Christmas reels. And that is his daughter Serena by his side, the golden-haired girl with the big smile, and his wife Joyce tending to the musicians. They do the Christmas Dance the week before the great day and sometimes they fly to Kuhikuhikapapa'u'maumau and sometimes they stay in Chicago and once they flew to Looseleaf and walked out on the lake, the three of them, hand in hand, as the moon shone down and lit up the ice like a circus ring and there by an old shack with a Christmas star on the roof they stood and waited for the wolf to call from the woods and he did. A long joyous cry from the dark.

ABOUT THE AUTHOR

Garrison Keillor, author of a dozen books, is founder and host of the acclaimed radio show *A Prairie Home Companion* and the daily program *The Writer's Almanac.* He is also a regular contributor to *Time* magazine. His latest novel is *Pilgrims.*

The employees of Thorndike Press hope you have enjoyed this Large Print book. All our Thorndike, Wheeler, and Kennebec Large Print titles are designed for easy reading, and all our books are made to last. Other Thorndike Press Large Print books are available at your library, through selected bookstores, or directly from us.

For information about titles, please call:

(800) 223-1244

or visit our Web site at:

http://gale.cengage.com/thorndike

To share your comments, please write:

Publisher
Thorndike Press
295 Kennedy Memorial Drive
Waterville, ME 04901